A PONY OF OUR OWN

Jean and Stuart Donaldson have
always longed for a pony of their
own, so they set about earning the
money to buy one. They are lucky
enough to find their ideal pony,
Kirsty, a black Highland mare; and
all their spare time is spent schooling
her, teaching her to jump, pony-
trekking, and, most important of all,
practising for their first gymkhana.

D1494983

Gillian

Douglas

PATRICIA LEITCH

A pony
of our own

Illustrated by Constance Marshall

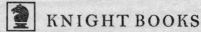 **KNIGHT BOOKS**

the paperback division of
Brockhampton Press

ISBN 0 340 03757 1

This edition first published 1971 by Knight Books,
the paperback division of Brockhampton Press Ltd, Leicester
Second impression 1974

Printed and bound in Great Britain by
Cox & Wyman Ltd,
London, Reading and Fakenham

First published 1960 by Blackie & Son Ltd
Copyright © 1960 by Patricia Leitch

To Meg

[1]

STUART, my elder brother, knelt on the kitchen floor and counted the money. 'Seventy-nine pounds, ninety-four pence,' he said.

When I asked him afterwards what he had been thinking about while he counted the earnings of the last seven months he said: 'Mostly the glorious thought of never again having to get up at five o'clock on a winter morning to deliver papers to sordid houses.' All I could think about was that at last we had enough money to buy a pony. Only those of you who have spent barren years spectating at gymkhanas, or plodding on foot after a fast disappearing hunt, will really understand the joy of that moment.

It was the result of a particularly disastrous afternoon at our Pony Club.

After much persuasion we had borrowed Blossom from our unwilling milkman. Blossom is nearly fifteen hands, of uncertain age but definitely aged, steel grey, hogged and docked and built, as the milkman put it, for comfort rather than speed. We arrived at the rally to find we were to be instructed by a Major Gryffe-Stobbings. Miss Knuttal, who was hardened to our arriving on strange mounts, was nowhere to be seen.

It was my turn to ride as Stuart had hacked Blossom from the milkman's yard. With a sinking heart I rode Blossom into the paddock where the Major, perched on a shooting-stick, was telling the other members to ride round in a large circle at the walk. I joined in and Blossom, her ears pricked at such lunacy, plodded round. In front of me Janet Dalton rode her part-bred black gelding with the ease of one who has ridden since infancy. Behind me I could hear Robert Morrison muttering elementary principles to himself, 'Heels down, hands still, look up,' he murmured while Copper, his obliging chestnut mare, walked out with a swinging stride.

'Right,' said the Major. 'Prepare to halt. Halt.'

For the good of my riding I applied what I hoped were the correct aids and to make Blossom stop I said, 'Whoaa lass,' in milkmanish tones. Blossom continued as if she hadn't heard. Her common sense told her that there was no point in stopping where there was no door at which to deliver milk. I took a strangle-hold on the reins and repeated my milkman imitation.

'That girl on the heavy grey,' shouted the Major. 'Would you mind stopping? Keep your hands still and drive your horse into her bridle with your legs and seat.'

Blossom set her neck muscles, tucked her head almost between her knees and shambled on. Well, I thought bitterly, if I do nothing else, I amuse the Pony Club. The Major was beginning to lose his temper. Forsaking his shooting-stick he strode towards us and made a grab at Blossom's bridle. Probably the sight of my feebleness at being carried away at the walk had made him more hasty than usual, and to Blossom a raised hand meant a blow. She gave a lumbering shy and broke into a fast, jarring trot.

Round and round we went, scattering ponies and riders. Scarlet with heat and embarrassment I pulled desperately at the reins and whoaed in a deep voice. I could vaguely hear the Major shouting instructions in the background as we clattered past. Someone on a bay horse suggested pulling her into the hedge. I pulled with both hands on one rein, and kicking wildly with the opposite leg I turned her into the hedge. She stopped with a bounce and I sailed over her neck to land head first in amongst the hawthorn.

The first thing I saw when I extracted myself and regained control of my scattered wits was the furious form

of the Major. In a voice icy with scorn he asked me to leave the paddock. Never before, he said, had he seen such a disgraceful exhibition. He hoped that I would never attend another Pony Club rally on a horse over which I had, so obviously, no control, and that much as he wished to encourage horsemanship in the rising generation, he could not tolerate such madness.

Praying that the ground would open and cover my shame, I led Blossom to the paddock gate. As I fumbled with the latch I heard a high, loud voice exclaim: 'But what can you expect riding a carthorse? I never saw anything so ridiculous.' The elder Leggat girl was laughing with a blond boy I didn't know. Turning her bay hunter she rode at an elegant extended trot across the paddock. Her riding clothes were immaculately tailored and her black hunting cap had never known mud.

She's sitting too far back, I thought spitefully. I had reached the depths. Why should I struggle on and on, never improving? I would never ride again but spend my days knitting and keeping my hands clean. Surely any fool could knit?

9

By this time Stuart had the gate open. 'Buck up,' he said. 'Let's go back the long way.'

'O.K.,' I agreed. 'Wait a minute and I'll loosen her girths. We'd better lead her until she cools down a bit.'

Stuart looked at her lathered sides and nodded. 'I'll take her,' he said.

We walked in silence. No words could express our feelings. I scratched Blossom's neck and hated myself for making such a fool of her. She was a jolly good milk-cart horse. Slowly we walked homewards.

At last Stuart spoke. 'Today was the utter end,' he said. 'We can't go on like this.' I wondered what he was going to take up instead of knitting. 'We're a standing joke with everyone in Tarentshire who knows the front of a horse from the back. "The Donaldsons, who are desperate to ride, haven't a horse and when they do manage to beg, borrow or steal one are too feeble to stay on."'

'We just have no chance to improve with one ride a month and then only to the blacksmith,' I added.

My miserable self pity must have been very evident in my voice because Stuart straightened his shoulders and continued in a completely different tone. 'And it's no good moaning about it. Action is what we need. We've got to do something about it. I rather think that if you hadn't had such a dead pull on Blossom's mouth you could have stopped her, and you were miles out of the saddle.'

'It's easy to criticize from the ground,' I muttered.

Stuart ignored me. 'I think she is cool enough to ride now,' he said, and tightening the girths he mounted. 'Of course our desperate need is money.'

'Obviously!' I answered. I was still smarting from his remarks about my heavy hands and bad seat.

'Enough to buy a pony so that we can both ride every day,' Stuart continued. 'I'm fourteen and you're nearly twelve. We've a whole winter in front of us and we jolly well ought to be able to make enough between us.'

I looked up at him and saw a familiar gleam in his eyes. All notions I had had of a winter spent lolling in front of log fires or tramping the countryside with the dogs vanished. We were going to make money. We were going to buy a pony. I thought of the Major and the Leggat girl's scornful expression and suddenly I felt like shouting, 'Up the Donaldsons!' and running full speed down the road.

The lower we go the higher we bounce. I think we must inherit it from Daddy who, although he sinks to the depths of depression, always rises again with his ideals intact. I dare say if your father is something in the City and frightfully rich, or even a prosperous farmer, you will be wondering why we didn't dash home and beg our doting parents to give us a pony. But actually that would have been useless, because Daddy, although understanding, is not doting and believes in his children making their own way in the world by the sweat of their own brows. Also he is an artist, which means our family finances depend upon how recently Daddy has sold a picture, and at the end of last summer we were going through a bleak patch while Daddy struggled with a portrait of an elderly Mayoress.

I will not bore you with details of our winter. We did not make our money by saving the children of millionaires from drowning and being instantly rewarded with fifty pounds, nor by finding strayed, prize-winning dogs or kidnapped children. It was a long, hard process which took all our Scottish determination to see us through.

Stuart delivered papers before school and dug gardens and delivered groceries after school. I spent evenings watching crying babies while their parents danced or shut themselves up in a cinema. I dragged fat, unwilling cairn terriers and asthmatic bulldogs for long walks, but I was unsuccessful as an errand-girl. Somehow I kept delivering the wrong parcels at the wrong houses and the time taken to correct my mistakes cut the profits drastically.

We had decided on the end of March as our time limit. So on March 31st we emptied our earnings on to the kitchen floor and while I sat with my fingers crossed, Stuart counted.

'Seventy-nine pounds, ninety-four pence.' He sat back on his heels and added, 'I should think we could buy a pony for that.'

'Goodness yes,' I said. I wanted no doubt to spoil the crowning of our efforts. 'We've the milkman's saddle.' This although old was a good shape and had been kept in reasonable condition by our exertions with neat's-foot oil and saddle soap.

'Right,' said Stuart, we stop making money and start buying a pony. I'll put the money away and if we hurry I should think we've time to take the advertisement down to the newspaper office tonight.'

I went to look for the sheet of paper on which, neatly written out in its final form, was our advertisement. We had wrangled a good deal over the wording. I had wanted to add 'No dealers', but Stuart thought this ridiculous as there were no dealers anywhere near Dunstan. He said that a reliable dealer with a reputation to maintain was far less likely to swindle you than a private owner selling one horse. Stuart had wanted to make the height fifteen hands, but I thought we would be better with something smaller and tougher. He won over the dealers, and I won over the height. So the finished advertisement read: 'Wanted riding pony about 14 hands; sound, used living out, moderate price.'

We cycled in to Dunstan and left the advertisement at the local newspaper office. The girl there gave us a box number and told us to call back in a week's time. We also borrowed instructional horse books from the library so we could swot up and hope to recognize the more obvious horse diseases.

Then we cycled back home through the deserted lanes. My bike is like an aged mare who has had many foals and suffered much hardship. Stuart's is a fiery, all steel, badly broken thoroughbred who does not respond to the free-wheel aids and is inclined to unseat one by getting behind the handle bars and losing contact with the pedals.

As we toiled homewards the clear saffron and ice green

of the Spring evening faded to grey. Dusk crept up behind the still, bare trees. Suddenly a few stars were visible and when I looked back at Dunstan it was diamonded with street lamps and lighted windows. An owl dropped from a tree and flew into the darkness without a sound. We were nearly home.

Our house is six miles from Dunstan, which is our nearest shopping centre. It stands in overgrown grounds hiding its grey-stone walls behind high, gaunt elms and gnarled oaks. It is very old and spreads sleepily in all directions. Inside, the rooms are small and strangely shaped with low, beamed ceilings and broad seats by the leaded windows. Dark passages run everywhere, dropping sharply with worn steps and twisting away mysteriously. I love our house. I think there have always been happy people living in it; people who know that home is the safest place in the world and the best.

As we left our bikes in the shed Stuart asked, 'Do you realize that our pony is somewhere at this very moment?'

'Gosh, no I hadn't,' I exclaimed.

I ran up the path to the back door picturing a grey pony lying like an enormous moth in the hedge's shadow, or a dim, grey shape standing with his head over a barred gate, his neat ears pricked, waiting for someone to bring him a titbit.

But as it turned out I was quite wrong.

NEVER have I known a week pass so slowly. From one Thursday to the next seemed years. Stuart and I talked of nothing except the pony, and I honestly believe I thought of nothing else.

Roland, my eldest brother who had just won a scholarship to Oxford, is an acute case of unhorsiness. He refused to stay in the same room as us but disappeared whenever he saw us, muttering that it had taken civilization centuries to produce the combustion engine but his closest relations had to go grubbing back to Man's earliest form of transport.

Stuart and I both go to day schools in Dunstan. I go to Dunstan Grammar School and Stuart to a rather superior boy's school on the outskirts of Dunstan. There are three boys chosen from the Scholarship entries to go to Stuart's school every year and much to our amazement Stuart was chosen from his year. When I sat I just managed to scrape through my exam and secure a place at the local grammar school, but two boys with brains are quite enough for any family.

When Thursday arrived at last I arranged with Stuart to meet him after school so that we could collect the replies together, but fate was against me.

I was sitting in a corner of the classroom quietly dreaming about a bay hunter whose owner had to go abroad and who was willing almost to give his horse away as long as he had a good home, when I became aware of an enraged Latin mistress standing over me.

'I have asked you twice for the ablative form of *puer*,' she exclaimed, 'and twice you have assured me that you are certain you could provide a horse with a good home. Kindly be outside my door at four o'clock.'

When I arrived home at six o'clock I was met by a furious Stuart who had waited over an hour, but very sportingly had brought the replies home unopened. There were three letters and we read them by the study fire while we ate hot buttered toast and drank steaming cocoa.

The first was from Sir James Campbell of Rennellcraig and read:

Dear sir,

With reference to your advertisement in the Dunstan Chronicle of the 2nd inst. I have a chestnut gelding, nine years, 14 hands, which might prove suitable. If interested, please phone Dunstan 498 any evening between six and seven.

'But we can't possibly go to Rennellcraig,' I said. 'Why it's so grand they would drive us out of the grounds if they even caught a glimpse of my jodhs.'

'Don't be daft,' said Stuart. 'He's frightfully sporting; I've seen him at meets. Anyway nothing looks worse than brand new jodhs, and all we'll see is the very lowest stable boy.'

'Even the lowest stable boy at Rennellcraig would be too much for me,' I replied, unconvinced.

Neither of us liked the sound of the next letter. It came from stables we had never heard of on the other side of Dunstan, which was surprising because we thought we knew every stable for miles around and had mucked out and cleaned tack at most of them. The stable had two ponies for sale, one of which they were sure would prove just what we were looking for. We were invited to go and try them any time.

'Ugh!' said Stuart squirming, 'what a way to end a letter – "Yours, in anticipation".'

The last reply was from a Mr Young who merely stated in a fine copper-plate hand that he had a pony which he had been thinking of selling for some time and that

Sunday afternoon would be a convenient time for us to call and discuss the matter.

'And that's that,' stated Stuart. 'They will all want hundreds for their animals and treat our seventy-nine as a joke.'

Daddy came in and read the letters and we persuaded him to phone Sir James for us. An anonymous voice answered, went away to find out and then said that Saturday would be quite suitable for us to see the pony.

We thought we would manage to see both Sir James's pony and the ponies at the riding school in the one afternoon, leaving Sunday free to visit Mr Young.

Saturday dawned with a cloudless sky which banished my fears of being forced into my plastic mac by Mummy. After lunch I struggled into my ancient jodhs. and pulled on my polo-necked sweater which Mummy had given to me at Christmas and which was still fairly respectable. I combed my straight, black hair, wishing for the millionth time that it would show some tendency to wave instead of straggling so.

Stuart was waiting at the foot of the stairs. He was wearing one of Roland's old sports jackets with his jodhs. and looked seventeen anyway, and frightfully superior. As we ran for the bus he grumbled about my slowness and I guessed that he wasn't feeling as superior as he looked.

Sitting on the bus I had the most awful needle.

'I can't remember a thing,' I said to Stuart. 'They could sell us anything. I'll never recognize splints or spavins or ringbone and how can anyone tell whether a horse has been exercised for hours beforehand to calm it down or given buckets of bran to hide broken wind. Sir James's horse probably has filled legs and has been standing all morning in cold water bandages.'

'We're not actually going to buy today,' said Stuart, 'only look. They can't make us take anything we don't like.'

We got off the bus and walked for about ten minutes

before we saw the gates of Rennellcraig. My needle got worse than ever.

'I think there is a side gate,' Stuart said.

'Let's look for it then. I feel it would be a sacrilege to leave footprints on those gravel paths.'

We found a tradesmen's door in the high stone wall and went in. A man who was weeding flower beds looked up and told us we wanted the path to the right.

'We're really here at last,' I said and started to sing. My needle had quite gone.

'Don't make such a din,' growled Stuart irritably, 'and for goodness sake be your age.' He was being very elder-brotherish.

The stable buildings consisted of eight loose-boxes and what appeared to be grooms' quarters, all built round a gravel yard. As we approached, five heads peered over half doors, ears pricked at the sound of our voices.

'Oh, look Jean!' cried Stuart, 'a palomino. I'm sure she's an Arab.' Her dark eyes were set wide apart in her dish face.

'She is rather sweet,' I murmured rubbing behind her ears.

'Aye, miss,' said a voice at my elbow making me jump. 'Best little Arab this side of the border.'

The voice belonged to a small, hard-bitten man wearing gaiters, a checked waistcoat and a green, pork-pie hat. Stuart introduced himself and said that we had arranged to see the chestnut pony Sir James had for sale.

'Aye,' said the little man, 'I've had instructions to show him to you. I'm Masters, his Lordship's groom.' He stood and stared at us with dark, gimlet eyes and then turned and led the way to the last loose-box. 'A right nice little pony. His name is Cracker. Just what you want for the Pony Club. A bit of feeding and he would carry you out hunting with the best. Sound as a rock he is. Never put a foot wrong and we've had him five years now.'

The pony was a light chestnut with a white blaze and

socks. He was finely built and seemed higher than fourteen hands. While the groom went to fetch the tack we spoke to Cracker, but he laid his ears suspiciously and ignored us. The groom returned and saddled and bridled Cracker. He was to be ridden in a twisted snaffle and tight standing martingale.

Out in the Spring sunshine he appeared a very washy chestnut indeed and I thought a trifle long in the back. When Masters tightened the girths Cracker swung his head round with bared teeth, but Masters was expecting this as he had a tight hold on the off rein and said something to us about this pony being no slug.

Masters led Cracker down to what had once been a sunken garden but was now converted into an outdoor school. Stuart was offered the first ride but he refused, saying he would like to see the pony ridden round first. Masters mounted and walked Cracker away from us, then trotted him back. He had even paces but struggled continually against the martingale, poking his nose out and lowering it only to jerk it up again as far as the martingale permitted. Stuart signalled to Masters to take Cracker round again and he cantered round twice.

'He's not really what we're looking for,' I said to Stuart.

'No,' he agreed, 'but he is nice. I'm sure he would show as a small hunter.'

'I don't know. Do you not think he's a bit ewe-necked? All the books say that's a bad fault.'

Stuart rode next while Masters stood by me and praised the pony. Certainly he went very well. He had a low, daisy-cutting movement at the canter. Stuart had him moving well up to his bridle and was taking him round in large circles.

'Right, Jean,' Stuart said dismounting, 'your turn.'

It was wonderful to be riding something different from milkmen's or greengrocer's ponies. Cracker was so much narrower and felt so gay beneath me. He obeyed a very light aid and I rode a moderately successful figure of eight

18

at the walk and slow trot. Then I cantered round and walked him back to Stuart.

Masters was looking most annoyed and Stuart was saying, 'But that's nonsense. The pony can't possibly be tired. We must try him in traffic because we shall be hacking in traffic quite a lot.'

Masters turned to me and said in disagreeable tones, 'Your brother wants to try him on the roads so you'd better hop off and let him on.'

'Jean can ride,' said Stuart. 'I just want to see him in traffic.'

Masters grunted and led the way out to the road. Cracker walked out well and I patted his sleek, shining neck and wondered if he would ever belong to us. I rode on, leaving Stuart and Masters standing at the gates. It was a quiet road and at first only two cars passed us. Cracker took no notice of them but trotted on.

Suddenly there was the sound of something heavier approaching. Cracker stopped dead. He ignored my aids completely. I had lost contact with his mouth and felt as if I was trying to push on a block of wood with my legs. He poked his nose in the air and listened. A lorry came into sight round the corner in front of us. Cracker let out a piercing whinny and went straight up. Somehow I managed to throw myself forward on his neck, but I slipped back in the saddle. He struck out with his fore legs at the empty air, touched the ground for a moment and went up again. For seconds he was balanced almost vertically while I hung on with my arms round his neck. My face was buried in his mane and the pungent smell of frightened horse was all about me. Then he plunged down, swung round and galloped off in the opposite direction.

Once I'd regained my seat he wasn't difficult to stop. I'm ashamed to say I dismounted and held him while the lorry crawled past. The driver shouted apologies and I shouted back that it was my own fault and thanked him for stopping. I led Cracker back to Stuart and Masters.

'Are you O.K.?' Stuart shouted.

'Perfectly,' I replied.

'You stuck on jolly well.'

'Rubbish,' I said. 'He didn't go very high.'

Masters took the reins and said he had never known that pony do that before. Huh, I thought, that explains the wretchedly tight martingale.

'I'm sorry to have taken up so much of your time,' Stuart said, 'but neither my sister nor myself are experienced enough to tackle a rearer.'

He sounded rather pompous but Masters didn't say any more. We thanked him for all the trouble he had taken and said good-bye. Scowling, Masters led Cracker away.

'Thank goodness you remembered about traffic,' I said.

'Mmm,' said Stuart, 'but anyway I rather think he would have wanted a lot of money for him. I'm sure he would have shown.'

'They knew perfectly well he was a rearer, yet they would have sold him to us without a qualm.'

'Poor Cracker,' replied Stuart. 'When I'm rich and a superb horseman I shall buy nothing but difficult horses and remake them.'

We had to catch two more buses before we eventually reached the riding school. A broken board pointing down muddy lane told us it was ahead. The buildings at the end of the lane had a general air of neglect and disrepair. There was no one about, so we had a look round.

On one side of the weed-infested yard were four narrow stalls. Their floors were sparsely covered with soiled straw and were so sloping that they must have been misery for a horse to stand in all day. On the other side was one fairly roomy loose-box and a barn-like building divided into several small stalls. In one of these an aged Exmoor was standing, resting a forefoot. We scratched her neck and fed her pieces of bread from our pockets but she seemed too disheartened to take any notice.

The muddy lane we had come by seemed to go past the yard so we decided to follow it. It was thickly imprinted

with hoof marks so we thought the horses would be somewhere down the path.

On our right, as we left the yard, was a small, bare paddock with one rickety jump and an ancient Shetland
hobbling round, his feet turned up with laminitis. We
were arguing about whether the Shetland could enjoy its
life when down the lane came the returning ride.

Without exception all the horses were on the forehand.
They moved forward at their own dragging pace while
their passengers giggled and talked to one another. Some
were sitting on the cantle of their saddles, their legs thrust
forward, their reins hanging in loops, whilst others were
almost on the pommel, their legs far too far back, hanging on by their reins with a dead stranglehold.

Two horses were most pitiful. They were both dark
bays and each step they took seemed a terrible effort to
them. Their sunken quarters, staring coats and protruding ribs spoke only too plainly of scant feeding and
neglect. Their dull, lack-lustre eyes held no hope, only
infinite sorrow and patience. The ponies, although poor,
were not in quite so miserable a state but all seemed in
need of shoeing and grooming. There was a black with
two wall eyes, a cobby chestnut with broken knees, a
bright bay whose mane had obviously been hogged with
scissors and a thirteen hand skewbald who still retained
enough traces of spirit to struggle to free his mouth from
the vice-like hold of his rider. They passed us, the riders
staring curiously at strangers in riding clothes.

I turned my head away, surreptitiously blowing my
nose. There was a hard lump in my throat. Whatever
happened I must not cry. Don't be so soft, I told myself
digging my nails into my palms, but the thought of the
bay horses and the awful life they must go on living and
the torture inflicted on them by anyone who could pay
out the price of a ride filled me with black misery.

'Come on, there's no point in going back,' said Stuart
with unusual tact. 'I think if we follow this path it will
take us on to the road.'

When we reached home the family were agreeably understanding about our unsuccessful horse coping and Roland said it was better to travel hopefully than to arrive. But somehow our travelling didn't seem very hopeful.

[3]

WHEN I woke on Sunday morning I lay in bed still half asleep, trying to think what day it was. The weather had changed. The wind was howling round the house and lashing the rain against the windows. I stretched and remembered it was Sunday and that we still had another pony to see. If he is anything like Cracker, I thought, I might as well stay here. The rain meant a battle with Mummy over the pink plastic mac and as it was Sunday she would almost certainly refuse to let me out in Stuart's old raincoat which is what I usually wear. Pink plastic, I thought disgustedly, feeling for my slippers with my feet.

When I got downstairs I discovered that it was only half past seven and as no one else was up I made myself a mug of coffee and tossed up whether I should make tea and take it up to the family or take the dogs for a walk. The dogs won.

We have three dogs. My Father's Dobermann Pinscher, Nero, who worships Daddy and barely tolerates the rest of us, Flirt, a golden cocker spaniel and Vixen, a black labrador.

I found Stuart's old raincoat, pulled on my wellingtons and tied a scarf over my head. I asked Nero if he would like to come with us but he only gave me a disgusted look and tucked his nose back in between his paws. Flirt and Vixen were already at the door wriggling with pleasure at the unexpected outing. We went over the back wall, through the woods and down to the river Torrance. The dogs dashed everywhere giving sharp, excited yelps and scrabbling in the dead leaves after the smell of rats and rabbits.

23

The Torrance was in spate. It flowed along a cold, icy grey, bursting into white foam over underwater rocks. I wondered where we would look next if today's pony proved unsuitable. Idiotically I had thought that if one had enough money it was the simplest thing on earth to find a pony. I stood for a while with my hands in my pockets staring at the angry waters.

We had arranged with Mr Blair, a local farmer, to graze our pony in a field which stretched down to the river and in return we were to help him at harvest time. Every morning we would come the way I had come this morning bringing bread, apples or carrots to our pony. What pony? I thought peevishly, digging into the soft mud of the river bank with the glistening toe of my wellington.

Suddenly I realized that Flirt was no longer with me. Vixen was waiting patiently beside a stick beseeching me to throw it for her but Flirt was nowhere to be seen. I called and hunted for her for almost twenty minutes and at last she appeared carrying half a loaf in her mouth. She looked downcast when I scolded her, but seemed to think she had done rather well for herself.

Mummy was exceedingly annoyed when I returned late and soaking wet. She made me dry the dogs and put them to their boxes and then gobble down cold bacon and eggs, telling me all the time that we should all be late for church because of my thoughtlessness.

We *were* late for church which made Mummy more annoyed than ever. She insisted that Stuart and I wait for Sunday lunch which is a long drawn-out affair. Roland had disagreed with the sermon and kept arguing with Daddy about it and making everything slower than ever. Stuart and I waited impatiently.

'We'll be seeing ponies in the dark if you don't all hurry up,' I muttered.

'Ponies, ponies, ponies,' mimicked Roland. 'You'll be eating grass yourself soon and lashing out every time anyone speaks to you.'

'Oh, hurry up, Roland,' I said.

'Patience is a virtue worth cultivating,' remarked Daddy, with raised eyebrows. 'The chair you are sitting on came from an acorn that came from an oak that grew for long, still years in a forest; and coal that you use every day without thinking has lain for centuries in the cold earth of time.'

'I haven't centuries to lie anywhere,' I said, 'but at the rate you move at in this house we'll soon all be fossilized.'

Mummy said, 'Don't be cheeky, Jean,' and Stuart kicked me under the table which meant 'for goodness sake be quiet and let them get on.' I scowled and pushed my hair back.

'The shaggy pony shook back her remarkably straight mane and pawed the ground,' mocked Roland.

I could think of nothing sufficiently cutting to answer back. I hated his exact, sarcastic voice. For a second of rage I stared at him then I picked up my tumbler and threw the remaining water at him. As always when I lose my temper my aim becomes remarkably accurate. An astonished Roland sat dripping with water.

'Well, of all the things,' he spluttered.

'I think you had better go to your room, Jean.'

Daddy's cold voice brought me back to my senses and I ran out of the room and upstairs to my bedroom.

I sat on the window seat and stared out over the cold, wet world. I had spoilt everything, absolutely everything. Surely no one else of nearly thirteen threw glasses of water over their brother merely because they were annoyed. I pictured myself going through life getting worse and worse until I ended up by shooting someone who had dared to disagree with me. It was very cold and despite my Sunday-best tweed suit I was shivering.

Downstairs I could hear them washing up. Roland came to the back door and let Vixen out. He didn't melt, I thought and immediately thought that thinking that proved I wasn't in the least sorry. Then I heard Stuart coming upstairs three at a time.

'Honestly, Jean, you are an idiot,' he said, coming in. 'We'll need to wait another hour for a bus now. We've missed the half past two one.'

'I don't suppose I'll be allowed to come,' I said.

'Well, you've to come down and apologize so I should think you've a pretty good chance.'

I tackled Roland first. 'I'm sorry,' I said.

'And I should just think so, too,' he replied.

'I didn't mean to do it. I lost my temper.'

'It's high time you started to control that temper of yours. When I think of all the things you've thrown at me! – and you always seem to hit me.'

'I really am sorry,' I said again.

'Oh forget it,' he said and laughed, 'but do me a favour: keep away from axes when I'm around.'

Mummy said she despaired of ever improving me and Daddy gave me a lecture on self-control.

'Can I go with Stuart?' I asked.

'Yes,' said Mummy, 'but you're not to change.'

'But I can't go like this to see a pony. Whatever would the owner think?'

'It's that or nothing,' said Daddy.

'And you're to put your pink mac on,' added Mummy.

We caught the half past three bus, myself tastefully covered in pink plastic and still wearing my suit. The bus run to Mr Young's was long and very peaceful. The road wound its way along the banks of Loch Dorach. The waters of the loch lay still and grey mirroring its many islands. Gradually the rain stopped and small patches of blue sky began to appear.

We got off at the village given in the address and asked our way to Mr Young's. The man we asked pointed out a white farm house sitting fairly high on the mountainside. We thanked him and followed the road up to the farm. I took off my plastic mac and carried it rolled up into a small bundle.

The farmyard was pleasant and prosperous looking. The farm buildings all looked in good condition and the woodwork had recently been painted in dark, glistening green and through an open barn door we could see the brilliant scarlet of a tractor.

Stuart knocked on the farm door. 'Either they are so rich they won't want much for their pony, or they've become rich through making enormous profits on all their deals and will want a hundred and fifty pounds for a Shetland,' he said.

Before I had time to answer him the door was opened by a red-cheeked young woman. 'Yes?' she said.

'We've come to see Mr Young about a pony he has for sale,' said Stuart.

'Och, come away in then. It would be you had the bit in the paper. Father saw it and we thought it would be a rare chance to be getting rid of the greedy wee thing. Eating her head off she is and doing not a thing for it.'

We followed her through a long narrow scullery to a large kitchen. It was a lovely room, warm and welcoming; the low beams were hung with bunches of drying herbs; the red tiled floor, covered with rag rugs, gleamed softly in the firelight; there was a shining black range and a blazing fire; on the walls were strings of horse brasses – but best of all were the photographs of ponies and cobs which hung all round. In almost every one the animals were proudly bearing prize tickets or rosettes and a little man in a hard bowler was standing at their heads or mounted or driving them.

'Dad,' said the young woman, 'here's two children to see you about the pony.'

In an armchair by the fire a figure I hadn't noticed before stirred and sat up.

'I'll be making you a cup of tea,' went on the woman. 'Just be sitting yourselves down and don't you be believing all Dad will be telling you. He's an old man and aye likes a bit blether about the past.' She went out, banging the door behind her.

'Aye, sit yoursel' doon,' said the voice from the chair. I saw him now more clearly. He was the little man in the photographs. His bright blue eyes took in everything about us as they flashed over Stuart and myself, but his face was old and sunken and the blue veins stood out on his wrinkled hands. 'Our Lizzie has a tongue you could sharpen a scythe on but she's guid at heart. She doesna' mean a thing. And you're wanting a pony?'

'Yes, sir,' said Stuart.

'Aye, it would be for yourselves?'

We nodded.

'You'd be the artist's children from over Dunstan way?'

'How on earth did you know?' I asked in astonishment.

'Och I kent your faither when he was a bit laddie. She's a nice wee mare I have. I bred her myself five year ago. She was the last. After that there jist wasna' the room to keep my stallion. He'd to go. You'll have heard of him maybe, Rory of Dorach?'

Even I had heard of him. He must have been one of the most famous Highland pony stallions in the West of Scotland. That finishes it, I thought. Any foal of his would be worth far more than eighty pounds.

'I'd to sell him in his prime, and many's the firsts he has taken at the Highland since he left me.'

'How terrible having to sell him like that,' I said.

'It was, but there jist wasna' the room. Like a son he was to me. As gentle a one as you'd find anywhere. I've seen the day when I had near forty ponies and cobs and now I've but the twa. My auld mare who'll no go till I'm deid, and Rory's daughter. I thocht she would make the fine pony for the bairn but she's feart, terrible feart, and it's no richt a young pony like that, full o' life and kindness, no doing a thing all the day but eat.'

The door opened and his daughter came in carrying a tray.

'Come along, Father,' she said, 'drink this and hurry up and take the young people up to see the pony or it'll be so dark it won't be tonight you'll see her.' She bustled us through our cups of tea, then saw the old man was well wrapped up before chasing us out of the front door of the farm. We walked round the side of the farm, then through a gate and followed a track up the mountainside.

'You've plenty grazing here for Highlands,' said Stuart.

'Och, it's Lizzie's man. All he thinks about is tractors and his sheep. It fair grieves his heart to see ponies about the place at all.' Mr Young stopped, whistled a long piercing note: 'They'll hear it and come,' he said. We listened in the silence that followed and almost at once we heard the pounding beat of hooves on the short mountain grass.

The ponies appeared a little above us, standing alert on a rocky outcrop of grey stone.

'Ponies come up then. There's the wee lassies,' called Mr Young.

They stood for a minute, heads held high, suspicious of Stuart and myself. Then sure-footed as goats they trotted down to us.

The old mare was nearly pure white. Her long, light lashes fell over her dark eyes as with ears pricked she snuffled with delicate nostrils in Mr Young's pockets.

The younger mare was still unsure of us and waited a little way off. She was jet black against the grey-green grass. She stood almost fourteen hands high, four square and as hard as the land which bred her. She was well coupled up with grand sloping shoulders and quarters like a ship's cook. Her legs were straight with long forearms, short cannon bones and flat knees. She stood with her hocks well under her, balanced on large, open feet of blue horn. Her neck was short and powerful and covered with rough, unkempt mane reaching down her shoulders. The arab blood which is in all Western Isle Highland ponies showed in the high carriage of her tail, her small pricked ears, large eyes, slightly dish head and fine curved nostrils. She was rough, muddy, heavily coated after a winter spent on the mountainside yet every line of her body spoke of her breeding and quality. I was conscious of the immense power contained in her compact body yet her dark eyes were more gentle than those of any other pony I had ever seen.

She stepped slowly forward, her flared nostrils showing scarlet. I spoke quiet, meaningless words to her and held out bread. She took it with velvety lips blowing on my hand. Stuart offered her a bit of bread too and she stood snuffling over us while we rubbed her withers and neck.

'Oh she is lovely, lovely, lovely!' I exclaimed. 'She is exactly the pony I've dreamed about.'

Stuart scowled at me and I remembered about never

praising a horse you are hoping to buy because of putting the price up.

'Here,' said Mr Young, 'put this bit rope round her neck and we'll take her down to the yard and you can try her. She was broken in last summer by the son of an old friend of mine. No trouble she was; jist explaining to her what you wanted was all there was to it. But she's green running wild all winter like that. Never had one person to ride her and take her about gentle like to see things and get used to them. Not the thing at all, at all.'

Stuart slipped the rope around her neck and she came quietly with us. The white mare followed a little way behind, then, realizing she wasn't wanted, turned away and began grazing.

In the yard Mr Young took the worst of the mud off the pony and then saddled and bridled her. 'Take her into yon wee field and ride her round,' he said to Stuart pointing the way as he spoke. 'Remember she's green and go easy with her.'

She stood quite still while Stuart mounted, then walked out with long strides to the gate. She was wearing a snaffle and a very loose standing martingale.

'I aye like a strap on a young pony's head jist so they never find out their heads can go up,' Mr Young said when I remarked on the martingale.

'It's very loose,' I said.

'Och she doesn't really need it,' he replied.

Stuart took the pony round the field using his legs and making her walk out. Then with a touch of his heels he put her into a slow trot. He took her round in circles, changing the rein several times and frequently altering the pace from walking to trotting and back again to a walk. Then he cantered her round twice and brought her back to the gate.

At the walk and trot she had moved well, stretching herself at the trot and coming back into hand at the walk but at the canter she seemed heavy in front and unbalanced.

While Stuart was riding a girl of about seven or eight had joined us at the gate. She was a pale, fat child with blonde ringlets.

'Is that your brother on the pony?' she asked.

'Yes,' I answered sharply. I didn't want to talk. I wanted to stare and stare at Stuart riding the black pony so that I would never forget them. The pony carrying herself so proudly yet with the staying power of her breed able to go on for miles and miles without tiring and the tall, dark boy urging her forward. Years ago Stuart's ancestors must have ridden ponies just like this one and I imagined them wrapped in their thick tartans, crouching close to their pony's shaggy necks as they guided them silently through a winter night on some wild border raid.

'She is a horrible beast,' said the little girl. 'She bit me once and Grandaddy made me sit on her back and she tried to run away and I fell off.'

And I'll bet you cried, I thought, ignoring her.

'Terrible feart,' murmured the old man.

Stuart dismounted. 'She *is* very green,' he said. 'And she is inclined to pull at the canter.' I knew he was trying to find faults in an attempt to bring down the price.

Mr Young turned to me and asked, 'Will you be having a wee ride?'

'Oh I can't. I've a skirt on.' I said longing more than anything to be astride the pony and see her rough neck and prick ears rising in front of me.

'Och there's no one here to be minding that. On you go with you.'

I was through the gate in a flash. I gathered up the reins and put my foot in the stirrup. Then suddenly I knew I mustn't ride her. I wasn't wearing jodhs. as a punishment. If I rode in a skirt I would be cheating. I took my foot out of the stirrup. Blast my conscience, I thought.

'I can't,' I said to Mr Young.

'Ooh, she's scared too,' said the little girl.

With as much dignity as I could muster I explained why I couldn't.

'Threw the water over your brother did you now,' said Mr Young. 'Imagine that! Well you'd better turn the pony out again. I'll be leaving you to do it and be seeing you after.'

We unsaddled the pony who wasn't in the least hot and led her back to the mountainside. She stood looking after us as we left her before she turned and galloped away, her mane and tail flying. She's perfection, I thought, but I'll never see her again. I knew without a doubt that she would be far too expensive for us even to consider. We couldn't discuss the price because the granddaughter had attached herself to us like a clam and was telling us how trying her grandfather was, always talking about the ponies he used to have. We asked her what she liked doing and she replied, 'Reading comics,' and started telling us about her favourite comic strips, which was a little better than listening to her infantile criticisms of her grandfather.

When we got back to the farm, Mr Young had returned to his armchair.

'And you managed fine?' he said, and told his granddaughter to be running along now. She went sulkily and we heard her telling her mother that we never read 'Merry Capers'.

'Then you like my wee mare,' said Mr Young.

'Very much,' replied Stuart. He had obviously stopped being a hardened horse dealer. 'She is just what we are looking for.'

'You'll not be finding a better.' The old man sat staring into the fire sunk in thought and I wondered if I would ever know half as much about ponies as he did.

At last Stuart asked the question we had all been avoiding. 'How much are you wanting for her?' There was a moment's silence that seemed to last for hours.

'It's not money alone would buy her from me. I could get more than a hundred pounds for her any day but like your sister my conscience would be bothering me. I'll let you have her for ninety.'

He was making a sacrifice but it was wasted on us. 'I'm afraid the most we can afford is seventy pounds,' said Stuart.

'Och, lad I canna go as low as that. Eighty-five I might consider but not seventy.'

'I'm sorry,' said Stuart. 'We just haven't got it. It has taken us all winter to make seventy pounds and we simply must have a pony for this summer.'

The old man said nothing. There was nothing more to say. I'd known from the beginning that this must happen. Stuart apologized for causing so much trouble and with leaden hearts we got up to go.

Mr Young nodded good-bye from his chair. He seemed suddenly very old and I hated Time that had turned the man in the photographs with his beautiful ponies into this tired, old man doomed to live with a son-in-law who worshipped tractors.

We walked away from the farm. 'I knew whenever I saw her she was too good for us,' said Stuart.

'Oh, she was lovely,' I said dismally.

'A mare by Rory of Dorach. We might even have shown her at the Highland,' sighed Stuart wistfully.

'Look there's that beastly granddaughter and she's running. Let's hurry, Stuart, or she's going to catch us up.'

We pelted along and as we reached the main road the bus came sweeping round the corner. It stopped for us and we jumped on.

We spent the journey home imagining horrible names for the granddaughter. We giggled loudly at our suggestions. It stopped us thinking about where we were going to look next for a pony, while every turn of the bus wheels took us farther away from the black pony. We'll never see another one like her, I thought. She was the loveliest pony there could possibly be. And I suggested Delilah as a granddaughter name.

We reached home about nine o'clock. 'What are we ~ing to tell them this time?' I asked.

'~ ~nows,' Stuart replied.

34

'Lord knows,' Stuart replied.

Roland was out but Mummy and Daddy were sitting by the fire in Daddy's study.

'No luck again?' Daddy said.

'How did you know?' I asked gloomily.

'Your faces,' said Mummy and I realized she was laughing.

'It's nothing to laugh about,' I said.

'Go on, Greg,' said Mummy. 'Put them out of their misery.'

'Well,' said Daddy, 'about half an hour ago your Mr Young phoned and said he was too old now to let twenty pounds stand between anyone and happiness. He said there weren't many girls as honest as my daughter and you're to collect the pony next Saturday.'

I couldn't believe my ears.

'You mean the pony's ours?' yelled Stuart.

'I can't believe it, Daddy,' I shouted. 'She's the loveliest pony you ever saw. Are you absolutely sure he said that? I couldn't bear it if you've got the message mixed up.'

'I'm absolutely certain,' stated Daddy.

The black pony was ours! She would stand in the field by the river, we would ride her up the drive to the house, we would see her every day of our lives. The long summer months stretched gloriously before me.

'We've got a pony, a pony, a pony at last,' I sang, and the family said if I must sing would I mind going upstairs and singing there.

[4]

On Wednesday after school we went to the saddler's in Dunstan. It is a vast shop crowded out with old harness which was used when all the transport in Dunstan was pulled by heavy horses. The huge collars bleed their stuffing and the thick leather is now dry and cracked. Mounted and hanging on the wall is the stuffed head of a hunter, very mothy with protruding glass eyes. Stuart and I imagine all sorts of interesting past histories for the head but no one really knows the truth. Our saddler, Mr Duncan, is a tall thin man perpetually moaning about the unhorsiness of the present-day world.

We bought a second-hand bridle with a thick eggbutt snaffle bit, a rope halter and a dandy brush. Mr Duncan was very interested in our pony and asked us to bring her down and let him see her one day. We promised we would and he gave us an old ex-railway body brush for luck.

We cleaned the bridle at night with neat's-foot oil which improved it, but it was still very dry when we had finished so we soaked it well in the oil and left if till Friday night.

We all had long discussions on what to call the pony. Mummy suggested conventional names like Black Beauty, Midnight or Darkie. Daddy's names were more suitable for racehorses than for a Highland pony. His favourites were Abonita, Lady Go Lightly and Blithe Spirit. Roland's suggestions were howled down by everyone. We've-made-it, No Alternative and Knacker's Joy were examples of his weak wit and poor taste. Stuart and I agreed that it must be something Highland but neither of us could think of anything that suited her.

We went round the field she was to have, looking for holes to be filled in or barbed wire lying in the grass and telling each other gruesome tales of ponies that tore themselves to pieces on wire within minutes of being turned loose. We dragged branches from the wood to strengthen the weak patches in the hedges. It is rather a nice field, long and slightly sloping, reaching down to the river. There is a lean-to shed at the top surrounded by several oak trees which provide ample shelter from flies or cold.

On Friday night I wiped the bridle clean and polished it up with saddle soap till it looked quite shiny. Hanging it up I felt rather pleased with the result and was carried away enough to try and do something about my jodhs.

Stuart joined me and we were both applying stain remover in an attempt to appear smarter than usual when Roland came into the kitchen carrying two boxes. He gave one to Stuart and one to me.

'Buck up and open them,' he said. 'I can't wait to see you with them on.'

I tore my box open and there under masses of tissue paper was a black hunting cap. 'Roland!' I cried in delight. 'Oh Roland, thank you!'

Stuart's was the same. 'That's absolutely terrific. I've been wanting one for years,' he said. 'Thank you very, very, much.'

Roland brushed away our thanks. 'Oh forget it,' he said. 'It's nothing really.'

We tried them on in front of the kitchen mirror. Stuart suited his. With his lean, brown face he looked like the popular image of a hard man to hounds. My long, straight hair rather spoilt the effect of mine. When I'm older, I thought, I shall wear it taken up.

'So I went into the shop,' Roland said, 'and asked the man what he would advise as presents for two horse-mad children. I was going to buy you riding sticks but the man said had you hard hats and I said I didn't think so. He said he would suggest them because his son had been in bed for days with concussion all because he hadn't had one on. So I came home and measured your hats for size and there you are.'

'They must have cost the earth,' I said. 'Where in the world did you get the money from?'

Roland went the odd pink shade he goes when he is really embarrassed.

'Well, actually I've had a poem accepted and in a way it was about horses so I thought I'd spend the money on you two.'

'Oh, Roland,' I cried, 'how marvellous for you.'

Stuart ran to tell our parents and the evening turned into a rather wild celebration of this new Donaldson talent. Stuart and I wore our hunting caps all through it which added a gay, unconventional sporting note.

It was very late before we went to bed and quite late before we got up on Saturday morning. We had planned to set off early and to take turns riding home but it was ten o'clock before we eventually got away and well after eleven before we were walking up the road to the farm.

'I shall remember this day for ever and ever,' I said looking down on the little village and the sparkling waters of Loch Dorach. 'For years we'll say "Remember the day we brought the black pony home", and it's happening now, this minute. Surely in all Scotland there is no one as lucky as we are?'

'For goodness' sake,' said Stuart, 'don't start being wet so early in the morning.'

But my spirits were too high to be squashed by Stuart's scathing words.

In the farm yard Mr Young was waiting for us. We thanked him for his wonderful kindness but it was impossible to put into words what we felt.

'Och there,' he said, 'it's not in words you'll be thanking me but in giving the wee mare the home she's deserving. I've brought her in for you and given her a bit rub over.'

He led the way to a loose-box and inside was the pony.

It was a most glorious feeling to see her again and to know that this time she was our own. Her shaggy winter coat was shining and her tangled mane and tail had been brushed out until her mane hung almost neatly on the off side and her tail fell like silk to below her hocks. Her feet had been cut back and oiled and they shone blue-black beneath her feathery fetlocks.

'Kirsty lass,' I said to her and she looked up as if she knew the name.

'That's the real Highland name to be calling her,' said Mr Young. 'Kirsty dubh, the black Kirsty.'

'We'd thought of it,' said Stuart, 'and when you see her again it suits her. There's a wee Kirsty girl,' and the pony blew over his hand inquiringly. He went into her box and bridled her. She stood quite still while Stuart adjusted the bridle, then he led her out into the yard.

I gave Mr Young our seven ten-pound notes. He stood looking at them as they lay in his hand and I knew he was thinking the pieces of paper were a poor exchange for the last pony he had bred himself.

'You'll be taking good care of her,' he said. 'Just remember she's but a wee lassie and take her gently and you'll no be going far wrong. Well, you'd best be getting on your way. It's a fair step to Dunstan.'

Stuart handed me the reins and gave me a leg up. We had decided to ride home bare-back to save us carrying the saddle in the bus.

'Good-bye sir,' called Stuart. 'We'll bring her over to see you sometime, if we may, and thank you again for your wonderful kindness.'

'Yes thank you very, *very* much,' I said. 'Good-bye.'

Mr Young stood and watched us go, and turning to wave to him I would have given anything to know what he was thinking. As we left the farm, Kirsty whinnied loudly and an answering whinny came from the grey mare who was watching our progress from the mountainside.

Kirsty was very comfortable to ride bare-back. Her

thick coat was warm and soft so that you couldn't feel her backbone at all. She took a great interest in everything we passed, pricking her ears and peering at anything unusual. At first she was fresh and inclined to jog and shy at anything moving in the hedgerows but she soon settled down to a long, striding walk. She was fearless in traffic and passed double-decker buses and a lorry piled high with shaking planks of wood with only a flicking of her ears to show that she noticed them.

I think I enjoyed the ride home more than any other before or since. Riding bare-back you are so much more a part of your mount than when you are riding with a saddle. The sun was shining on the smooth waters of Loch Dorach and Kirsty's unshod feet made hardly any sound on the soft dust of the roadside. I was completely happy.

For a little time all my earthly desires were satisfied. My head was full of plans for the summer; wonderful, impossible plans.

We stopped and ate sandwiches while Kirsty grazed by the loch side. Then I trudged behind while Stuart rode the rest of the way home.

We were surprised to find Roland waiting at the field gate. He seemed disappointed that we hadn't come off and needed the protection of hard hats.

'She's not very big,' he said, 'What's going to happen if Jean grows immensely fat?'

I made a face at him and said we had decided to call her Kirsty.

'I once knew a washerwoman called Kirsty,' Roland said, 'she wasn't much of a washer but a nice old soul all the same.'

I imagined Kirsty looking benignly out from under a white cap, her front feet all crinkly with the hot water.

'Are we going on up to the house?' I asked Stuart.

'No,' he said, 'I should think today's the longest she's been ridden and she's pretty soft coming off grass like that. We'll turn her out for tonight.'

I led her into the field and took her bridle off. She shook herself like a huge dog, then cantered away, lay down and rolled, then started grazing.

'That's fine,' said Stuart, 'she's got her head down. She'll settle O.K.'

We acted the fool going home – leap-frogging through the wood, talking all the time in frightfully Oxford accents to get Roland into training for his future conversations. Life seemed very good that evening.

After supper Stuart and I took bread crusts and carrots and made our way through the damp grass back to her field.

There were two cows in the field with her which were company for her yet saved the awful struggle of keeping one pony in a field while trying to take another one out, which would frequently have happened had there been another pony in with her.

She was grazing close to the cows but walked to us when we called and held out the bread. She ate our offerings and followed us back to the gate hoping for more.

'We've been absolutely, terrifically lucky,' I said to Stuart.

'Umm, she is very nice. It's strange for ponies the way you buy them, and they know nothing about it till someone they've never seen before appears and takes them away.'

'We'll never sell you,' I whispered to the listening pony, but the darkening night made Stuart more realistic. 'You can never tell,' he said, 'no one ever knows what is going to happen in the future.'

March flowed slowly into April and April turned gently into May. The days grew warmer and longer. No more was it a cold, dark duty to ride in the morning before school but the most delightful time of the day, filled with birds singing and untarnished with people coming and going, the sky a pale far blue and the trees the very new green of another Spring. Sometimes there was only myself and Kirsty, our progress leaving dark trails in the dewy grass; other mornings Stuart would come too and I would sit on the gate watching while it was his turn to ride.

We hacked nearly every day, one riding and the other cycling, the pony beneath us filled with bustling self-confidence at taking us somewhere. We walked her on the tarmac roads and trotted along the lanes, soft and muddy with spring rains. She hated high hedges and many times I had to dismount and pull her out of the opposite hedge, cursing my foul horsemanship that had allowed her to get up the bank, while she stated most emphatically, with heaving sides and goggling eyes, that the other hedge held a horror that no horse could have been expected to face.

We schooled her about twice a week in a corner of her field, watched by the mildly curious cows. We read instructional books but neither of us really understood the theories of cadence and beat and we decided that the basic principle was to make her go forward freely and comfortably. We worked her on a small circle as this acted as a control, checking any unasked-for speed and making her bend her spine. She was very one-sided and we circled her twice as much on the right rein as on the left in an attempt to counteract this. We worked mostly at a slow, sitting trot. If allowed to go faster she was inclined to loose her head and at a walk she lost impulsion very easily and plodded with her head drooping.

Her moods were many and often exasperating. When she felt like it she would treat schooling as a huge joke which she understood far better than we did. She would trot briskly round with a smug expression on her face. Her backing and turns would be competent but uninspired as though she were humouring us at a stupid game which she was playing to keep us happy. On her bad days she would stubbornly refuse to circle, trying continually to take us back to the field gate.

She had a most definite pony character with strong likes and dislikes. She hated farm workers and we heard

42

from a friend that one of the labourers from Mr Blair's farm had been bucked off twice when he tried to steal a ride. She loathed rain and baulked when ridden into it, moving unwillingly along her head almost facing the opposite direction.

By the end of May we told each other, in our more optimistic moments, that she was improving, that she was becoming more supple, that her halts were more balanced and her backing and turns smoother and less reluctant.

There were no mounted rallies of the Pony Club since we had bought Kirsty and it was not till the beginning of June that I had a chance to ride her with more than one other horse.

[5]

FOR most of my life any unknown girls I happened to meet at home were invariably Roland's girl friends. They were usually arty types who held long discussions on life after death, or the fate of mankind, or modern art or poetry. A mouse scared them into hysterics, they wouldn't cross a field with cows in it and, although they declared that they utterly adored dogs, they seemed happier when Flirt, Vixen and Nero were in another room.

It was a very pleasant surprise, therefore, when he produced Sara. She was tall and slim with fiery red hair and Roland said she had been more or less born in the saddle. Daddy said how amazing, and she didn't sound quite Roland's type. Roland replied that her riding was altogether different from Jean's and Stuart's grubbing about in a muddy field with a fat pony, and that when Sara had lived in England she had ridden at Windsor and Olympia and hunted three times a week in the season.

I didn't see much of Sara until one evening, when I was rubbing the saddle mark off Kirsty before turning her loose, Sara stopped at the field gate riding a skewbald cob and wearing immaculate ratcatcher and a bowler.

'I've been up to your house looking for you,' she shouted. 'Stuart told me I would find you here.'

I let Kirsty go and she immediately trotted over to the gate. I followed carrying the saddle and bridle and wondering what Sara could possibly want with me. Kirsty was nipping at the skewbald so Sara dismounted and we walked back home together.

'Next week-end I'm going down to my aunt's at Chisturn and I wondered if you'd like to come too?' Sara said.

'I'm taking back a dressage horse I've been schooling for her and as my horse-box holds three I'm taking this fellow down as well and I thought you might like to bring Kirsty. My aunt runs trekking holidays so we could ride out with them.'

'That would be wonderful, Sara! I'd love to come,' I said. 'It's a super idea but won't it be frightfully inconvenient for your aunt having a strange pony and rider arriving out of the blue?'

'Oh, I said in my letter that I would probably be bringing someone but anyway she has a huge place down there and at the very most she only has six trekkers.'

'It will be jolly good experience for Kirsty. She's never been ridden with a lot of other horses.'

'Nor boxed?' asked Sara.

'Not so far as I know,' I answered.

'You'll need to watch she doesn't kick out at the other horses. Some Highlands kick like the very dickens to begin with. I was thinking of leaving on Friday afternoon and coming back on the Sunday evening. Could you manage that?'

'Well, we have games from three to five on a Friday but I'm so rotten at them I'm sure nobody would miss me.'

'Bring Kirsty over on Thursday night and I'll meet you outside your school on Friday at three. You needn't bring much. I'm going down in my riding things and that's all we'll be wearing when we're there, so it's really only night things you'll need.'

'Sara,' I demanded suddenly, 'did you ask anyone at home about all this?' I had an awful vision of Mummy saying, 'but of course you can't possibly accept'.

Sara laughed, 'Keep your hair on,' she said. 'I saw your father before I asked you and I told Stuart. They were both keen for you to come.'

We had reached my house by this time and were standing talking by the gate.

'I'll see you on Thursday night, then,' said Sara, mounting.

'Right. Thank you very, very much for asking me,' I called.

She put the skewbald into a trot and I stood leaning on the gate watching them go. The cob had a very short tail which he carried kinked over his back, making it seem shorter than ever. Sara hardly moved as she posted to the trot. She's going to get some shock when she sees me banging about on top of Kirsty, I thought, and then I wondered if I had been humbly grateful, and then if I hadn't thanked her enough.

As I dawdled back up the path, reluctant to go inside and start my algebra homework, Daddy appeared from the house carrying a sketch pad.

'Isn't it wonderful Sara asking me to go with her,' I said. 'Why do you think she asked me? She must have masses of hunting friends.'

'Oh purely because you're Roland's sister,' answered Daddy vaguely, settling down on the doorstep and starting to sketch an elm tree with a dead bough which reached gauntly to the ground.

Well, it's an ill wind that blows nobody good, I thought and went in to struggle with x, y and z's, my head full of the vision of strings of ponies cantering over short, rough grass, their manes and tails fanned out by a sea wind.

On Thursday night I rode Kirsty over to Sara's house, balancing an attaché case in front of my saddle. Kirsty's appearance was most satisfactory. She had lost all her winter coat and was gleaming like polished jet. I had had her shod on Wednesday night and we made a grand clatter on the hard roads. Sara's house is about half an hour's ride away and as I had promised Mummy that I would be home in time to wash my hair, I pushed Kirsty on, cantering on any soft going.

The house itself is very modern, red brick and turquoise tiles smothered with Virginia creeper, The front door was standing open but the only sign of life was a young Afghan Hound lying stretched out in the doorway. He lifted his head when we approached but decided we were harmless and let it drop back on to the rug again.

I was a bit doubtful about my ability to dismount and keep my hold on the case, so I called and a little plump lady with crimpy, grey hair came to the door. I asked if Sara was about and she said I must be the little friend that Sara was expecting and that she was in the paddock jumping Vanity, but if I went round the side of the house and down the little lane to the right I would see her. I thanked her and turned Kirsty.

But Kirsty who had been most obliging all the way there, whipped round in the opposite direction. I turned her again, forcing her on with my legs but she had no intention of going the way I wanted. Quick as a flash she turned and the next second we were in the middle of a rose bed. I felt her collecting herself for a buck and as I tried to keep her head up the wretched case fell from my hands, burst open and scattered its contents over the roses. Genuinely alarmed, Kirsty shied back on to the path leaving me sitting amongst the roses. Sara came round the side of the house to find me rising from the rose bed tastefully adorned with my striped pyjamas and my pony disappearing out of the gate.

'Good Lord,' she exclaimed. 'What on earth is going on?'

I picked myself up and tried to stuff my belongings back into the case. The little lady and the Afghan had both withdrawn, apparently quite unperturbed by the violent happenings in their front garden.

'I'm frightfully sorry,' I said. 'I was carrying the case and like an idiot I dropped it, Kirsty shied and I came off. I hope the roses are O.K.'

'Oh never mind the roses! Kirsty might be anywhere by now.'

And then to our complete surprise Roland came in the gate very gingerly leading Kirsty, who was nibbling at her reins in an absent-minded fashion.

'I say,' he shouted, 'did you come off on your head?'

'Oh Roland, where did you find her?' I yelled.

'This animal? Here take her, she has a look in her eye I don't like. I found her eating grass by the roadside. I thought I did rather well recognizing her.'

'The little horror,' Sara said. 'She must have stopped the minute she got out of the garden.'

I was too relieved to see her again to say anything and while I repacked my case they led the penitent Kirsty round to the stables.

When I reached the stables, which were three portable pelhams standing on concrete, Sara had unsaddled Kirsty. She was standing in a loose-box munching hay and looked as if butter wouldn't melt in her mouth. The little lady came round and Sara introduced her to me as her mother. She seemed to know Roland quite well already and told him it was like old times for her having girls sitting amongst her roses and ponies trotting off down the drive.

Sara said, 'Nonsense Mother, I always held on to my reins!'

I apologized again about the roses and wondered if I would ever be quick-witted enough to hold on to the reins. Then after saying good-night to the horses we all went in and had coffee and biscuits.

The next morning I packed my jodhs. in a large paper parcel and put an aertex shirt on under my gym tunic. After breakfast I said good-bye to the family. Stuart had been very decent about everything, helping me clean tack and groom and never complaining that Kirsty was half his. Even on the Friday morning he didn't seem in the least jealous and I felt a sudden pang of misery at leaving them all.

'I'll be back late on Sunday night,' I told them.

'We'll wait up,' Daddy promised. 'Be sure and enjoy yourself.'

'I'll try,' I said and wondered if riding a nappy Highland pony with Sara would be enjoyment.

On the way to school I talked Carol into taking the brown paper parcel, which would then contain my gym tunic, home for me.

'No wonder you're so rotten at games,' she said. 'You just don't try.'

'That's rubbish,' I said. 'Trying doesn't make you good at things. I try and try and try to improve my riding, yet last night I fell off at a tiny shy and let the pony get away.'

From two till three was English Poetry which normally I like but I could only think of whether I would manage to slip away before games and wonder if Kirsty had boxed easily.

'Where sits our sulky sullen dame,
  Gathering her brows like gathering storm,
  Nursing her wrath to keep it warm.'

read Miss Ballantyne and I imagined a furious Sara waiting in her horse-box until half past five.

After English there was the usual mad Friday afternoon rush to the games room. Everyone was clutching hockey boots or shorts, so my parcel didn't look as odd as it might have done. The girls with trains to catch were carrying their coats so no one suspected that mine was the sign of a planned breakaway.

Miss Drobbett, our games mistress, is a tall, angular woman with cropped hair who always wears long, black stockings and a ridiculously short tunic. She bounced into the changing room. 'Quickly, girls, quickly into cubicles and change. We don't want to waste a minute indoors when we could be out in the fresh air, do we?'

I shared a cubicle with Carol. As I changed into my jodhs. and wrapped my tunic up I made her promise not to say a word about where I was going even if my absence was noticed. She was beginning to get nervous and kept saying, 'You're not really going to do it are you?'

I pushed her out into the games room and stood listening behind the cubicle door. I heard Miss Drobbett marshal everyone into a line and then march them out of the games room. The door banged behind them. I counted thirty slowly to make sure no one was coming back then I tip-toed into the deserted games room. My jodhs. looked queer under my navy nap coat. If anyone sees me they're sure to spot them, I thought. Never before had I seen the games room completely empty and, strange though it may seem, the green tiles, the chromium plating and the rows of hockey sticks seemed weird and menacing.

Rapidly I shut the door behind me and with a shudder of irrational fear I ran round the corner of the gym and squeezed through a gap in the hedge on to the road.

I had done it! I was free! and there at the end of the road was the huge mass of the horse-box. Sara, hearing my running footsteps, opened the cab door.

'Well done, Jean,' she said. 'I've been crossing my fingers for you.'

I scrambled up and slammed the door behind me. 'How did she box?' I asked.

'Like a lamb. No trouble at all.'

Sara released the clutch and we swung round into the main road in front of my school. There to my absolute horror, stood Miss Drobbett watching from the kerb while my form crossed in a single file.

'Sara,' I almost screamed. 'It's my form!'

Quick as a flash, Sara picked up her bowler which had been lying on her knee and jammed it over my head. 'Scowl,' she said. 'Don't look at them.' For an eternity they walked across the road till at last Miss Drobbett with a cheery wave to the driver of the horse-box and her strange companion joined the end of the file. Sara started up the engine and we were safe.

'Crimes!' I said, emerging from underneath the bowler. 'I can't think what they were doing there. They should all have been playing hockey by now.'

'That rat-like woman would have died if she'd known who was in here,' Sara said.

'If she had recognized me she would have been up here in a minute and have dragged me down to the hockey pitch by the scruff of my neck.'

Riding in a horse-box gives one a glorious sense of

power due to the height of the cabin, the muffled movements of the horses behind one and the excitement of going somewhere with horses. I said this to Sara but she only laughed and said she dreaded to think how many precious hours of her life had been spent in horse-boxes.

Sara drove smoothly and easily and soon the outskirts of Dunstan turned into open country; rough brackened country divided by crumbling stone walls and inhabited by sheep bleating piercingly and coated with matted wool. Curlews cried mournfully and Sara pointed out a roe deer but it disappeared before I saw it. Many of the hills were covered with forestry plantations of pine and spruce. Sara said that the paths through them were wonderful for cantering and with any luck we would get a ride through them tomorrow.

It was six o'clock before we reached Sara's aunt's. We went up a winding drive to the stable block which had once been the home farm but was now the groom's house. Sara backed the horse-box into the yard and we both jumped out and craned down the ramp. Kirsty had been boxed last. She nickered when she saw us and came down the ramp with quick bouncy steps, then stood blinking in the daylight. The skewbald cob came next and stood with lowered head, blowing at the dust and shaking himself. I held Kirsty and the cob while Sara got the dressage horse out. He was a big bay animal, dark with sweat after his journey. He pawed at the floor of the box while Sara untied him and he slithered down the ramp in his anxiety to reach firm ground again.

A lady in an old tweed skirt, a massive double-knit pull-over and wellingtons came across the yard towards us. I knew at once that she must be Sara's aunt because of her flaming red hair.

'Hello Sara,' she shouted. 'Have a good journey? Goliath looks sweated up. Here I'll take Panda,' she said to me and took the cob.

'Hello, Paddy,' Sara said, as she reached the ground

safely with the bay. 'Jean, this is my aunt, Mrs Laird but everyone calls her Paddy. Paddy, Jean Donaldson and Kirsty Donaldson.'

We shook hands getting our halter ropes slightly entangled.

'We'd a grand journey,' said Sara. 'Where does Goliath go?'

'The last loose-box on the left. It's all ready for him,' replied Paddy and added that Panda and Kirsty were to be turned out in a field down the road but they would be fine in the paddock until after dinner. We turned them out into the paddock. Then, while Sara was rubbing down Goliath, Paddy showed me the six trekking ponies and her own Arabs.

'The trekkers arrive tonight for next week,' she told me. 'After dinner I bring them down and introduce them to their mounts. That's why the ponies are all in just now.'

There was a brown, half-bred Connemara called Maud; a bay pony of about fourteen hands with a very dished face called Shona; Donald, a heavy, dun garron of nearly fifteen hands with the expression of a worried nursemaid; a gentle, flea-bitten grey called Shadow; Snap, a bright chestnut of just over thirteen hands and a big black cob of the good old-fashioned type, both hogged and docked who was called Mutineer. Paddy had two Arabs, both dark dapple greys. They were beautiful horses and I could have spent much longer admiring them and feeling their velvety lips nuzzling my hands but Sara returned. She had settled Goliath and she said he was eating his feed and that she herself was starving and could eat a horse.

Paddy said that this was a vulgar suggestion in the present company but that dinner would be ready in half an hour so we had better go. We brought our cases out of the horse-box and followed her in.

Chisturn House was built from grey stone quarried locally. At either end were two towers with slit windows and in the middle of the turreted stone wall joining them was a massive, iron studded door. Green lawns rolled away from it, patterned with stiff, decoratively cut flower beds, bright with wall flower. Tall, dark pines grew shelteringly behind it. Everywhere houses like this were turning into hotels and boarding schools but here and there one lingered on, still someone's home, still linked with the horse who had made its long history possible. I looked at Paddy and wondered what it felt like to own anything of such age and dignity but she was talking to Sara about the price of oats.

I was given a little bedroom overlooking the formal gardens in the front of the house. I washed quickly and combed my hair and was ready when Sara knocked. We had dinner with Paddy and Brigadier Laird in their own oak panelled dining-room so we didn't meet the trekkers who had dinner in the long hall. It was a lively meal, disturbed by the activities of five Labrador puppies and a Siamese cat. The conversation was all of hunting; the runs, the falls, the good days, the bad days and the merits of horses and hounds. Sara said she would take me out next season, but I rather suspected that the attraction of Roland would wear a little thin when he went to Oxford.

After dinner Sara parked the horse-box in an old barn and we took our tack to the saddle room. The Brigadier came with us to show us the way to the ponies' field, his voice loud in the still June evening. 'Capital weather for this trekking racket,' he was saying. 'Went out with them once myself. Some of them don't know a horse's head from its heels but Paddy soon gets them going. Amazing woman, absolutely amazing. I remember when. . . .'

Kirsty walked alongside me, nudging my pocket hopefully. It's not possible that I was at school this morning and I'm here now, I thought, and I imagined Carol giving my brown paper parcel to Stuart and going home to their trim little bungalow to tell her mother about the thrills of today's hockey game. And I wondered yet again at how different people are.

6

NEXT morning we had breakfast with the trekkers in the long hall. It was a beautiful room with a high, raftered ceiling and polished wood floor. The sun shining through the stained glass windows made glimmering patches of purple and scarlet on the table.

Breakfast was very good. We had grapefruit, bacon, eggs, kidney, toast and marmalade and coffee. By the time we had reached the toast and marmalade stage our shyness had worn off and we had stopped being stiffly polite to one another.

There were five pony trekkers, three girls and two boys. One of the girls looked about nineteen. She was small and rather fat, with loose brown hair, very red cheeks, a high squeaky voice and a quick nervous smile. Her name was Alice Dunbar. She said she hadn't ridden for very long but that she was keen to improve. Sara told her that she wouldn't be able to sit down after riding all day and Alice, giggling, replied that she had a bottle of liniment in her case.

The other two girls were twins. They were exactly alike. Both were tall with brown eyes and their hair tied back in blonde pony tails. Their names were Jill and Dana Peters. They told us that they had a Fell pony at home but now they were both away most of the time training to be nurses she was turned out with other ponies on a mountainside. They were both rather afraid that they would never catch her again as she had been difficult to catch when in a field with only one other pony.

The younger of the two boys was fourteen. His name was Roger Darcy and he had never ridden before and was only learning now because his mother thought it was so nice to see a boy on a horse. She had sent him to Chisturn with his cousin Geoffrey 'to be broken in', as Geoffrey put it.

Geoffrey Darcy looked older than Sara and was inclined to boast of his achievements in show jumping. He had been televised jumping at The Horse of the Year Show and was rather peeved when Alice was the only one who thought she might have seen him.

After breakfast I caught up Panda and Kirsty while Sara helped Paddy with the trekking ponies. Both ponies were standing waiting at the field gate and allowed themselves to be haltered without any bother. I wondered if I should ride Kirsty and lead Panda. I thought I wouldn't and then I thought how disgustingly feeble I was and scrambled on to Kirsty from the gate. Both ponies were anxious to reach the other ponies at the stables so we jogged happily back without any trouble.

As we turned into the yard Paddy, wearing breeches and boots and carrying a dandy brush, came out of a loose-box.

'You young fool,' she shouted, 'what do you imagine you're doing?'

Actually I imagined I was being rather dashing, leading one horse while riding another, but I knew from Paddy's tone of voice that she didn't, so I slid off Kirsty and said nothing.

'See what that child was doing, Sara,' said Paddy, calling Sara out. 'Riding Kirsty in a halter and leading Panda. Anything might have happened. You'd no control whatsoever. I don't suppose you'd any idea how Panda would lead but you knew they were both young animals, didn't you?'

'Yes,' I said, 'but it seemed so feeble to walk.'

'Feeble,' Paddy snorted. 'You young things are all the same. If a dog had run out of the hedge in front of you, Panda would have shied and Kirsty bucked and then where would you have been? I'll tell you. Two ponies running loose with halter ropes dangling amongst their legs.

Broken knees and rope shy for the rest of their lives. Two good animals ruined, but what would you have cared? Not a damn so long as you weren't feeble. It's about time that you learnt that proper caution isn't feebleness.'

'Nothing has happened this time,' said Sara soothingly, 'and I shouldn't think Jean will do it again.'

'I shan't,' I said.

'Well, if you've learnt a lesson without maiming one of the noblest of all animals, I'll say no more but remember next time you think "Gosh, how feeble", think again and see if it isn't elementary obvious caution,' and Paddy strode off into the next loose-box.

I felt as though I had been thoroughly wrung out and cast aside. Sara came over and took Panda.

'Don't worry,' she said. 'It's the colour of her hair. She can't help it. She has just discovered that Roger has hardly been on a horse in his life before although this morning he said he had ridden quite a lot.'

She gave me her dandy brush and said she would get another one for herself. I worked hard on Kirsty, grooming her in long sweeping strokes and fanning out her tail until it hung like silk. I knew every word that Paddy had said was true and it helped my hurt pride to see my pony gleaming beneath my brush. I brushed out her mane, taking it over her neck and back again. Paddy passed and said with a cheery grin that she had meant every word she had said but that her bark was worse than her bite and that was a nice tail I'd done.

I tied Kirsty to a ring bolt in the wall and went to look for her tack. All the ponies had halters on under their bridles and all were saddled with loosely fastened girths. They stood in their loose-boxes, sleek and shining.

'I'm looking for my saddle and bridle,' I said to Paddy.

'Up there,' and she pointed to a saddle rack above our heads. 'I'm coming out with you today. Mr Scott, that's my groom, usually goes but he's taking one of the brood mares down to the Midlands and he won't be back till Wednesday.'

I saddled and bridled Kirsty, thinking that despite her sharp tongue I liked Paddy and was glad she was coming with us. It was going to be a warm day and already Kirsty was flicking her tail against the flies. I thought I would be fine in just my aertex shirt with my jodhs. and leaving Kirsty I went indoors to get my hard hat.

On the way back I met the twins and Alice who told me that the boys were down in the yard.

'I'm riding Donald and the twins are to go on Shona and Maud. Donald is much bigger than anything I've ever ridden before,' said Alice apprehensively.

In the yard Geoffrey was leading out Mutineer, the black cob, and Paddy was mounting Roger on Snap.

'Watch you don't give him a job on the mouth when you mount. Right, toe to the girth. Up you go,' and with a practised hoist Paddy had Roger in the saddle. Alice led out Donald and the twins Shona and Maud. The yard was full of movement and noise. Kirsty whinnied loudly and there was a general outburst of neighing.

'My stirrups feel too long, Mrs Laird,' said Alice helplessly.

'Keep your feet in the stirrups and take your leathers up one hole if you want to, but I don't think you need to,' replied Paddy, casting a professional eye over Donald and Alice. 'Sit well down in your saddle. Feel your girths everyone. We avoid girth galls at all costs, caused by pure carelessness, nothing else. Yours are much too loose, the girl on Shona. I know the pony better than I'll ever know you my dear, so you'll not have to mind if I call you Shona now and again,' and as she spoke she tightened Shona's girths. 'Right. Take your ponies down the drive and back just to get the feel of them and then we'll be ready to start.'

The trekkers started off down the drive. The twins looked nice on their ponies, riding with balanced seats and a light feel on their pony's mouths. Alice was obviously scared stiff. She rode with her feet home and sticking out almost at right angles which brought her knees off the saddle and loosened her whole seat. Striving for security she clung tightly to the reins. But Donald was an old hand at the game and took her carefully after the twins. 'Give more rein,' Paddy called after her but she gave no sign of having heard.

Roger just sat on Snap with his reins hanging in loops. 'I can't make him move,' he said in a whiney voice.

'Kick him,' advised Geoffrey. 'Here I'll make him move for you. Get up you brute!' and he brought his crop down on Snap's unsuspecting quarters. With a frantic toss of his head Snap broke into a canter.

'Help,' Roger screamed, jobbing Snap in the mouth as he was thrown backwards by the sudden movement, 'Help me Geoffrey! Oh stop, stop! Oh please stop!' Bouncing around and in obvious danger of falling off, Roger was borne out of sight.

'That'll teach him,' said Geoffrey. 'I'm not going down the drive. Dash it all, I'm quite used to riding different horses. This old plug won't give me any bother.'

I left Kirsty still tied to her ring bolt and peering anxiously down the drive after the other ponies. I hate to hear any horse called a plug and I thought Mutineer looked a very honest workman. I followed Paddy and Sara into the saddle room. 'Mark my words,' Paddy was saying, 'Geoffrey will cause the trouble. You can spot them at once.' Then seeing me she stopped and asked me if I thought Kirsty could carry a saddle bag. I said I was sure she could and privately agreed with her about Geoffrey.

By the time I had tied the saddle bag containing sandwiches on to Kirsty's saddle and knotted her halter rope around her neck the trekkers were back.

'Shona is sweet,' said Jill, riding up. 'She has a super smooth trot.'

Donald with the same worried look in his brown eyes began to graze while Alice gave ineffectual little jerks at the reins. 'Oh dear,' she moaned, 'I'm afraid Donald has a will of his own. I do hope he's not going to be too much for me to manage.'

Roger, white in the face but still on Snap, said he thought his pony had run away with him.

'How soft can you get them?' said Geoffrey scornfully. 'You wanted to move, didn't you?'

'Don't worry, Roger,' said Jill. 'We all felt like that to begin with.'

'Everyone all right?' asked Paddy, riding up on Shadow.

'Of course this isn't the type of horse I'm used to,' said Geoffrey. 'I liked the look of those Arabs though.'

'I don't use the Arabs for trekking,' said Paddy sharply. 'Mutineer is as good a cob as you'll find anywhere. I don't think you'll have anything to complain about at the end of the day's ride,' and turning away from Geoffrey she spoke to Jill. 'Just keep an eye on Maud if there are any tractors. She's inclined to shy at them but if you're on the inside you've nothing to worry about. Sara, you know the way, take the lead please and if the boy on Snap will ride with me I'll give him some help.'

We made a very gay cavalcade through the village street. Mindful of Sara's warning I kept Kirsty at the back although she had shown no sign of kicking. She was excited with the company and inclined to jog but she seemed to be enjoying herself. I patted her sleek neck. 'You're the loveliest pony here,' I told her. 'I wouldn't change you for any of the others.'

We trotted on and Alice, scarlet in the face, bounced around on Donald's broad back. 'I can't manage to post,' she jerked out. 'He seems to go all ways at once.'

'Rubbish,' said Sara, 'you'll get it in a minute.'

'Look at old Roger,' shouted Geoffrey.

Roger, too, was having a rough time while Paddy said in hearty tones, 'Up, down, up down. Fit your movements in with his stride. Let the pony take you. Up, down, up down.'

Once through the village we turned off on to a broad

path leading over the mountainside. We followed it for about an hour and a half as it wound gently upwards. The ponies walked on loose reins, picking their way in the rough going.

We reached the top and there before us lay the sea, stretching far out until it joined mistily with the blue June sky. We seemed to be poised on the edge of the world with the land before us falling away to the sea and the sea stretching on for ever. Kirsty snorted, excited at the open space before her. I felt that if I had clapped my heels to her sides she would have taken wings and flown to the uttermost parts of the earth.

We continued slowly down the path as the ponies slipped a little on the loose stones. When we eventually reached the bottom, Sara stopped and, turning in her saddle, asked Paddy which way.

'Well I thought we would split up,' Paddy said. 'If you go through that gate you can cut across the open land and down the narrow lane to the point. You've been before. Tie the ponies to the trees and take the lunch over the rocks. I'll come round with Roger by the road.'

'Right,' agreed Sara and opened the gate. 'Will Alice be O.K. with us?'

'Yes, of course,' Alice said stoutly, but her face belied her feelings.

'Just take it easy. No mad, uncontrolled galloping and that means you all,' and Paddy's gaze rested on Geoffrey rather longer than on anyone else.

When we were all through, Sara shut the gate. 'You can see the lane from here,' she told us and pointed. 'We're making for there. I'll go first, then Alice, then Dana, then Jill, Geoffrey and you last, Jean. Space yourself out properly.' She trotted a few steps, then gently eased Panda into a canter.

Alice hung frantically on to Donald's reins and he backed into one of the twins but didn't kick.

'Oh, go on. Follow her,' said Geoffrey. 'You'd think it was some kids' riding school we were at.'

Alice loosened her reins a fraction and she was off at a jarring trot. The twins spaced themselves out successfully but Geoffrey followed on Jill's tail.

Kirsty was trembling beneath me but I was surprised to find that she didn't pull. I trotted her in a small circle, then galloped after Geoffrey. The salty wind blew past us making our speed seem greater. Before me the sea lay dazzling in the sunshine and above me the sky was an infinity of blue. The short, springy turf added buoyance to Kirsty's stride. I was riding my own willing pony and all my senses were sharpened and quickened with speed. I started to sing at the top of my voice but the wind tore the words from my mouth and threw them wantonly behind me.

In front of me Geoffrey had passed the twins and was urging Mutineer on. I saw Sara turn round and shout something I couldn't hear. Mutineer drew level with Alice and Donald. Geoffrey, using his crop, urged Mutineer to pass. They were neck and neck when Donald with a light-hearted buck broke into a lumbering gallop. Alice was

unseated by the buck and losing all control clung to Donald's mane. Sara pulled Panda in to a walk hoping, I suppose, that when Donald reached her he might slow down. They were nearly at the lane.

I was about three quarters of the way across the open land and could feel Kirsty tiring slightly. Her neck felt damp and she was blowing a little so I slowed her down to a trot.

Donald and Mutineer raced on past Sara until they reached the gate to the lane where they stopped, with Alice nearly off. Sara caught up with them and even from where I was I could tell she was angry. The twins caught up and they all went through the gate. Sara signalled to me to shut it and I waved to show that I understood.

Everyone disappeared down the lane. 'Never mind, Kirsty old girl,' I murmured, 'it's the oats that do it.'

Kirsty was anxious to reach the other ponies but I managed to shut the gate without dismounting and feeling rather pleased with her I turned down the lane. It was steep and narrow leading down to a grassy knoll covered with leafless, stunted trees.

Half-way down I could see the others. Sara was still in front holding Panda in to a very slow walk, then Alice and behind Alice, Geoffrey, then the twins. Geoffrey was riding right on Donald's tail. He seemed to be trying to pass which was almost impossible in the narrow track. The fool, I thought. He knows Alice has no control over Donald.

Then all at once it happened. Donald, excited after his race and pressed beyond endurance lashed out with both his back feet. I saw the glint of his shoes in the sunlight. I heard Mutineer's grunt, Alice's shrill squeal and Sara's voice loud with temper. Everyone dismounted and I put Kirsty into a trot. Before I reached them a white-faced twin passed me. 'I'm going for Mrs Laird!' she shouted as she cantered past. 'It's an artery.'

'Take the horses and get them away from here. They'll go silly with the blood. Good lord, Geoffrey, surely you can do that. Take Kirsty and see they tie them up properly,' Sara's voice was high and strained.

Geoffrey began to bully Alice and Jill into moving their horses and Panda. I handed Kirsty's reins to him. She shied and nearly pulled him over but he got her past.

It was Mutineer's off fore just above the knee. Sara swore at the departing figure of Geoffrey. She was gripping Mutineer's leg above the cut with both hands and pressing with her thumbs, while he stood with the piteous, helpless look of any hurt animal.

'I'm not getting it stopped,' Sara said. 'Oh pray that Paddy gets here soon. This is too much for me to cope with alone. If it had been Panda it would have been bad enough but someone else's animal! And I've absolutely nothing to make a tourniquet with.'

'Poor Mutineer,' I muttered then one of my few bright ideas struck me. 'I know,' I shouted. 'My hat elastic.' I wrenched it off my head, put my foot in it and pulled at the thick black elastic I had sewn on to go under my chin. It came away suddenly tearing the lining.

'Brilliant, Jean, I couldn't think of a thing.' Sara tied it round Mutineer's leg above the cut. 'Get a stone and I'll put it underneath the elastic where I think the artery is.'

We slipped the stone in and twisted the elastic tight with a stick. Slowly, very slowly the spouting stopped. It was still bleeding but not nearly so badly. As we crouched on the ground watching it I heard the sound of hurrying hooves.

'That will be Paddy,' I said to Sara, and because she was looking wretched I added, 'It was all Geoffrey's fault.'

'I was meant to be in charge of you all,' said Sara doggedly.

But Paddy had no recriminations. She jumped off her grey, tied her to the hedgerow and came over to us.

'Thank the Lord it wasn't broken. Oh good girls, you've got the bleeding almost stopped. I've phoned the vet. I should think it will need a stitch or two to get him home,' she said looking closely at the cut. She patted Mutineer, 'Poor old fellow. Not your fault I'll be bound.'

The bleeding was reduced to a trickle but when we tried to move him to the top of the lane it showed signs of worsening so we sat in the hedgerow eating sandwiches and taking it in turn to hold Mutineer. Dana and Roger were eating theirs at the top of the lane waiting to direct the vet when he arrived.

'He shouldn't be too long,' said Paddy. 'Luckily he was at a farm not too far away when I phoned. Now tell me how it happened.'

'We were all too close together in the lane. Geoffrey was pressing down on Alice and Donald kicked out,' explained Sara.

'Not like Donald. I expect you were racing over that open ground. Nothing but broken bones would teach some people a lesson and it's always the horse that suffers.'

'Here's the vet,' I said, thankful to avoid another of Paddy's lectures. He was quite a young man and came down the lane closely followed by Roger.

'It's a nasty kick,' he said as he looked at Mutineer. 'Have you far to go?'

'Chisturn House,' replied Paddy.

'Oh, you're the trekkers? I'll give it a stitch just to be on the safe side and an anti-tet. shot.'

He worked swiftly and efficiently. Roger was sent back to the car for a twitch but it wasn't needed. Mutineer stood without moving a muscle.

'Well, that's that,' the vet said, straightening up and giving Mutineer a slap on the shoulder. 'Nice cob. How old is he? Always give me a cob, I say. They'll be with you at the end when your blood horses are lying exhausted.'

'He's rising nine, but I don't agree with you about cobs. A good Arab would outlast any cob,' said Paddy decisively.

'Is that one of your party?' asked the vet. 'They seem to be everywhere.'

It was Alice toiling up the lane. 'Come quickly,' she called. 'It's Maud. She won't get up and Geoffrey thinks she's dying.'

'This is not my lucky day,' exclaimed Paddy. 'If you would come too,' she said to the vet. 'And Roger would you stay with Mutineer?'

We all ran down the lane and over the rough grass to where the horses were tied.

'She must have got loose,' said Dana. 'We heard her get down and roll and when we got to her she was lying groaning. Do you think she is poisoned?'

Suddenly the vet broke out laughing. 'Get her saddle off. That's the most important thing.'

Paddy and Dana undid the girths and pulled the saddle away.

'Now,' said the vet, 'see that branch above her hind legs? Pull it back. She has cast herself,' he said to Paddy. 'Rolled over and couldn't get up because of the branch.'

I watched with a tremendous sense of relief as Geoffrey dragged the branch back. I had been imagining Maud dying before our eyes and having to be buried where she lay.

The vet kicked Maud on the rump. 'Get up you wicked little varmint,' he said and with a side-splitting groan Maud rolled over and started to graze.

'It takes a native pony,' Paddy said. 'Cunningest little beggars you'll meet. Thank goodness she was only cast. One horse crocked up is quite enough for one day.'

'How's the saddle tree?' asked the vet.

'Feels O.K.' Sara replied.

'Right,' said Paddy. 'Saddle her up and we'll start for home.'

The vet said good-bye and we all thanked him. 'I'll keep my fingers crossed for you,' he shouted laughingly as he strode away.

I untied Kirsty, tightened her girths and mounted. It took a little time to round everyone up and when we were ready Alice discovered she had left her crop behind her on the rocks, which caused a further delay. But eventually we left Sara with Mutineer until someone could fetch them with the horse-box.

Meanwhile Paddy led the way home.

'You'll all keep your horses to my speed,' she said, 'and then I can keep an eye on you.'

Geoffrey was inclined to grumble but Paddy turned a deaf ear to him and we made our way slowly homewards listening to Alice's rather tearful and endless apologies.

After dinner Sara, Paddy and I went to look at Mutineer's leg. It was hardly swollen. He had finished his feed and was contentedly munching his hay.

'If that's pony trekking,' said Sara, 'give me a nice gentle point-to-point any day!'

'It has its moments,' agreed Paddy and left us to clean our tack in the warm, leather-smelling saddle room.

7

I AGREED with Sara that if we rode alone the next day we would probably get farther. Paddy thought this quite a good idea and said that the trouble with pony trekking was the different abilities of the riders. Sara said she would never have the patience to cope, but Paddy said it was amazing what one could do if one had to.

Sara woke me at the unearthly hour of six. I was more or less asleep but somehow managed to wash and struggle into my clothes. After three attempts I got my aertex shirt on the right way round and followed Sara down the back stairs to the kitchen.

Mrs MacIntosh, the cook, was up and padding about in a mauve dressing gown and a yellow scarf wrapped over the lumps of her curlers.

'Thank goodness you've come, Miss,' she greeted Sara. 'I've got four but the fifth I cannot find, hunt as I may.' I followed her gaze and there penned against the wall by a high wire fire-guard were four of the Labrador pups. 'Them four's to be taken out. The dratted girl don't come till eight so I have to do it. But I daren't let them four out of my sight till I've found the fifth.'

'He can't just have gone,' said Sara.

'Gone he has, Miss. There were five in this room when I went to bed last night and how many are there now?' and she glared suspiciously at the puppies behind the fire-guard as if daring them to turn into five. Then with a shrill scream she darted out of the kitchen.

'She's quite mad,' said Sara. 'I can't imagine what can be wrong with her now.'

It was too much for me at that time in the morning, so

I sat down on one of the wooden chairs and tried to resume my interrupted sleep.

The cook's head appeared round the door. 'It moved,' she announced cryptically.

'What moved?' demanded Sara impatiently. 'You know we really came down to see if there might be a cup of coffee.'

'That great, dirty rug,' said the cook. 'I told the Master when he brought it in last night. Rats, I told him, as sure as my name's Jinty MacIntosh.' And she stayed behind the door with only her head poking round it.

Sara strode across the room and lifted the rug with a flourish and there underneath was an almost suffocated puppy.

'Oh-h-h-h, imagine!' said Mrs MacIntosh, abandoning her refuge behind the door. 'I hung it up last night. Must have fallen slap on top of the puppy. Well I never did!' and she stretched out a brawny arm and deposited the pup with the others behind the fire-guard.

'And now,' said Sara, 'coffee?'

The coffee was blissfully hot and sweet, and by the time I had finished it I was properly awake at last.

We went out through the kitchen garden, climbed a wall into an orchard, and then through a gate which brought us out almost at the ponies' field. They were both lying stretched out on the grass, huge heaps of black and skewbald horse. Kirsty heaved herself up when she saw us but Panda waited with half closed eyes. Sara haltered him but he just sat up with a dazed, indignant look on his face. After a short lecture from Sara he condescended to follow Kirsty but he obviously took a dim view of the whole proceedings.

We had breakfast in the kitchen with Mrs MacIntosh, who told us all about her daughter who was doing so nicely as a shorthand typist. Personally I can think of nothing worse than sitting in an office all day banging a lot of little keys when there are such things as horses, dogs and the sea in the world, but Mrs MacIntosh assured us that her Barbara just loved it; ever so nice it was for her, she insisted. She packed up our lunches and told us to take care because you never knew with those great horses.

Paddy had given Sara an Ordnance Survey map and we traced out our route after we had finished grooming. We planned to go through the village and turn left, following a road over the hills for about eight miles and then a track along the side of Loch Hantry and come back through a forestry plantation which joined our original road about a mile above the village.

We tied our saddle bags on and mounted. Kirsty was fresh and I was stiff and it wasn't until my third attempt that I managed to scramble up. As we trotted past we waved to the trekkers who were having breakfast in the long hall. Geoffrey dashed to the window and shouted after us that we were jolly mean and that we might have waited for him. Sara assured him that she was desperately sorry, but pushed Panda into a canter.

We slowed down when we reached the road. The ponies walked well together arching their necks and striding out. Already the sun was beating down from an empty blue sky. It was going to be another glorious day.

We rode through the village where scrubbed children, waiting in their gardens until church time, rushed to their gates to see us pass and shouted, 'Ride 'im cowboy,' 'Here's the Cisco Kid,' and other such low remarks. Kirsty regarded them with such disgust that she had hardly finished shying away from one gate before it was time for her to shy at the next. I could feel Sara's pained gaze at my disgusting horsemanship and I was glad to turn up the road away from the village.

The road climbed through groves of larch and silver birch. Burns ran sparklingly alongside us, only to dive suddenly beneath the road and appear gurgling at the other side. Chaffinches flew from tree to tree with sudden spurts of flight. We saw a hare run long-legged from us, but no rabbits.

We dawdled with loose reins and our feet out of the stirrups, Sara telling me tales of her days at Richmond and Olympia. She had mostly shown hacks and children's ponies when she was younger. Really, she said, it was a question of the most money buying the best horse. She was not very keen on show jumping, thinking it too artificial and too crammed out with pot hunters, but she was very keen on three day events. She had ridden once at Badminton but her mare had strained a tendon in the cross-country and had been unable to compete in the final show jumping phase.

We talked on, the horse talk that varies so little yet is always new and of unending interest. There is no other talk like it in the world.

The scenery changed as we rode. Our way now led between high heather-coloured hills, sloping down to the road which twisted and turned in an effort to stay in the glen and avoid climbing their sides.

Sara was telling me about the Pony Club she had belonged to in England when without warning a man sprang up from the heather and ran towards us waving his arms and shouting. Kirsty gave a horrified snort, a buck and before I could collect my wits we were galloping gaily round the corner.

To my utter amazement the hillside was swarming with men wearing a scarlet tartan and brandishing claymores. On the road were cameras and long, gleaming American cars. Just as we rounded the corner somebody yelled, 'Shoot', and we were in the midst of a Highland charge. Kirsty stopped with a rubbery bounce and I sailed over her head.

'Cut,' yelled the same voice. 'Get that kid out of the way, someone. This'll drive me clean loco.'

A man with a megaphone boomed to the charging Highlanders to get back up that mountain.

Kirsty was nibbling the heather with a sheepish look and she allowed herself to be caught without any trouble. I turned to look for Sara and saw her talking to a little fat man in a grey and red check suit and the most frightful, shocking-pink tie. I led Kirsty over to them.

'That sure is just what we were looking for,' the man was saying. 'So cute all shaggy like that and that cute hair hanging all over its face.' I was appalled to think that he might mean Kirsty.

'This is her owner, Jean Donaldson,' said Sara. 'Jean, this is Mr Trenton.'

'Sure is swell to meet you,' announced Mr Trenton, pumping my hand up and down.

'And he was wondering if he could use Kirsty in his film,' continued Sara. Mr Trenton said that he was making a great epic film all about the '45 rebellion and he sure would love to use my pony in it. I was just about to answer with an indignant no when I saw Sara making violent faces at me. I made a face back, which was meant to convey that I didn't want to spend any more time than I could possibly help with a man who had called Kirsty cute and shaggy and referred to the last noble representative of the house of Stuart as if he had existed solely to have American films made about him.

Mr Trenton saw my face and inquired whether I had hurt myself when I had fallen off my pony and Sara said she was sure Jean wouldn't mind his using Kirsty. I knew then that Sara's face had meant 'say yes' and that she had no finer feelings about the ill-fated house of Stuart. I decided that as I was her guest the laws of hospitality compelled me to agree. So I said I supposed it would be all right, but that we couldn't be long as we were riding down to Loch Hantry.

'That's just fine,' said Mr Trenton and invited us to come right over and meet the gang. Unfortunately the Highland Charge had started again and the ponies stood rooted to the spot with goggling eyes. When we could get them to move again we were introduced to the gang.

There were three cameramen and a sound effects man who was there to absorb the atmosphere and would concoct the sound from records when he got back to America.

71

They all said, 'Hiya, swell to meet you.' There was a continuity girl, with a sheaf of papers in her hands who seemed desperately harassed and kept running around trying to make people listen to her. We were introduced to a tall, bald man who was the historical expert. I felt rather sorry for him because I was sure Mr Trenton would never let a mere historical detail stand in his way.

The star of the film who was to play Prince Charles was sitting alone in one of the slinky American cars. Mr Trenton whispered his name in awe. He said he was a great actor and they sure were lucky to have got him but he was just a little difficult and we wouldn't disturb him. Instead he left us with a glamorous red-head and went off to see how his charge was progressing.

The red-head introduced herself to us as Cora de Levan and told us that she was playing the great part of Flora MacDonald. Her eyelids were bright green and her eyelashes mascaraed into little black crescent horns. She thought the part of Flora was wonderful: the lonely maiden waiting for her prince to land from France, staying with him through the long weary days and escaping with him to happiness. I had been right about the historical expert.

Then she, too, left us. We sat on the hillside eating our sandwiches and holding the ponies' reins and letting them graze about us. Sara explained that she had always wanted to see a film company on location and that she had thought this too good a chance to be missed.

After the Highlanders had charged four more times Mr Trenton came over to us and said, 'Well I guess that's in the bag. How about some coffee?'

'What about filming Kirsty?' I asked.

'That'll be right next,' he assured me. 'But right now everyone breaks for coffee.'

'But the light?' said Sara.

'Oh that'll hold for a minute,' said Mr Trenton. 'Don't you worry. Just you come and have a cup of coffee.'

Leading rather reluctant ponies we followed him to a

group of people gathered round Prince Charlie's car.

'Here's the little horse I was telling you about,' said Mr Trenton.

'Oh gee, no,' exclaimed the star. 'I've not got to horseback ride now. What is it? An overgrown Shetland? And who is the kid anyway?'

Boiling with rage I looked round for something to throw at him. Luckily there was nothing within reach so I said in what I hoped would be County tones but which actually came out rather squeakily due to my temper, 'She's a pure bred Highland mare and not an it of any sort, and we were hoping to ride to Loch Hantry today if you would get a move on.'

'Keep your hair on, honey,' the star said. 'I wouldn't know a pure bred Highland mare from a scotty dog,' and the rest of the group laughed.

Mr Trenton gave us our coffee which was black and very strong and assured us again that it wouldn't take a minute once they got started. He pacified the star by telling him that he had no horseback riding to do and started to explain to everyone just how he intended to use Kirsty.

'It's like this,' he said. 'The Red Coats are searching everywhere and in the castle Charlie lies asleep exhausted. Who can get through to warn him? Only Flora knows where he is. She alone must do it. She disguises her beauty and, dressed as an old Scottish woman, leads her pony loaded with peats over the mountain to the castle. How's that? It's got everything – romance, danger and an animal.'

'There is no historical record of the Prince being rescued under those circumstances,' said the historical advisor in a mild undertone.

'It's what the public wants,' declared Mr Trenton in a final voice. 'I guess it's just one of those things that were never recorded but it sure is what the public want. Now, have we Miss de Levan's stand-in? That's it, darling. Are you all ready? That's swell.'

A girl rather like Miss de Levan had appeared wearing a long black skirt and well wrapped up in a tartan plaid.

'We are going to get this cute little pony all ready and you are going to lead her down the mountainside,' continued Mr Trenton.

'Oh gee!' exclaimed the stand-in. 'I ain't never touched a horse before.'

'Well now's the time to get acquainted,' said Mr Trenton in hearty tones.

A long, scarlet monster of an automobile drove up, a man jumped out, dived into the boot and produced two creels.

'If you'll just take the saddle off the pony,' Mr Trenton said to me, 'we'll get started.'

I unsaddled Kirsty who was very fed up with the whole business. She had her ears laid and was taking frequent nips at Panda. The man approached with the creels and Kirsty swung her head up and backed away saying she had never seen anything like them in her life before. She refused to stand while we lowered one creel over her back. Sara tied Panda to a tree and came to help. This shifted Kirsty's mind from the creels to the absence of Panda and she allowed them to be placed on her back while she whinnied desperately.

'That's just grand,' said Mr Trenton who had been watching the carry-on with a worried eye. He beckoned to the stand-in. 'Now you just take this pure-bred Highland mare up to those two trees and lead her down the mountainside. Take it easy. You're weary, worn out; each bush may hold an enemy.' If it did, I thought, you wouldn't hold Kirsty. 'Only you can save your Prince. Right take her up,' and he handed the stand-in Kirsty's halter rope.

The stand-in led away Kirsty who was sure that she would never see Panda again and whinnied long and loud. The poor stand-in looked as if she were leading a man-eating tiger but they reached the two trees quite successfully and stood waiting for directions.

Mr Trenton bawled at them through his megaphone to

go up a bit farther and appear from behind the trees. I sat in the heather watching with Sara.

'You're a desperate woman. Only you know where the Prince is,' roared Mr Trenton. 'Ready, shoot.'

The cameras whirred and Kirsty and the stand-in started down the hillside. They didn't look in the least like an old Highland woman and her pony weary from the peat cutting. They looked exactly what they were, a nappy young pony with the thought of getting her own way foremost in her mind and a girl who was scared stiff of horses.

'Cut,' yelled Mr Trenton. 'Take her back. You're in disguise, you're old, you've both had a hard day cutting peats but the real you is a valiant woman saving the man you love. You've got to bring it all out. Back you go.'

But Kirsty had other ideas. She had been moving in Panda's direction and that was the only direction in which she intended to go on moving. She dug her toes in and stood like a rock while the stand-in gave little ineffectual tugs on the halter rope.

'At this rate,' I said, 'we are going to have to run and go back when we get away from here. I'll have to go up and move Kirsty for her.'

'I'll go,' offered Sara jumping up I was quite content to let her go. The sun was warm and the heather a clean, good smell about me. Sara had only gone a little way when Kirsty got the better of the stand-in and they both trotted down to Panda.

I could hear the girl's high voice as she talked to Mr Trenton and the continuity girl. The sun beat down and I lay back in the heather shutting my eyes and letting it burn golden into my brain. I must have fallen asleep because I woke to find the stand-in sitting next to me.

'Goodness!' I exclaimed, 'what's happened?'

'I just couldn't budge that ornery animal and now look.'

Coming down the hillside were Sara and Kirsty. The

cameras whirred and it wasn't Sara any more but an old woman dragging her way home.

'Gee,' muttered the stand-in. 'She's good.'

'Cut!' boomed Mr Trenton. 'We'll take it again, slightly more to the right. Thank you.'

'She can make that horse do whatever she wants,' moaned the stand-in.

'She has lived with horses all her life,' I said, 'and Kirsty has far too much will of her own.'

'Sometimes I just wonder if I shouldn't have gone on being a stenographer even after I won that beauty contest. I guess I'd have been married with kids of my own by this time if I'd stayed.'

I didn't want to get mixed up with her life so I just sat and stared at Kirsty and said nothing. They shot her five times and then at long last they were finished.

While Sara changed I took the creels off Kirsty and saddled up. She was very cross and scowled all the time. Sara, dressed in her jodhs. once more, came and untied Panda.

'You were very good,' I called to her and she rode across grinning.

'It was terrific fun,' she said. 'Perhaps I'm cut out to be a stand-in. I'm afraid I've rather wasted your day.'

'A fat lot you care, I don't think!'

'You don't really mind, do you?' she inquired anxiously.

'Course not,' I replied, mounting. 'It's not everyone has a pony who has been in the fillums.'

'We haven't time to go right down to Loch Hantry, I'm afraid, but if we follow this track across according to the map we should join up with the forestry road.'

Mr Trenton came over and was gushing in his thanks. He took Sara's name and address and I wondered if this was the beginning of her rise to fame. Surprisingly he asked me for mine too. I gave it to him and decided he was just humouring me.

We rode away following the track and waving good-bye to the film unit. Even Prince Charlie condescended to leave his car and wave a languid hand.

We found the forestry road without any trouble. It was a broad path well coated with pine needles and stretching through the high, dark trees. We had a wonderful canter along it until we reached the road above the village. As we were later than we had intended to be we trotted briskly on and through the village, pulling in to a walk about half a mile from Paddy's.

It was well after four by the time we had unsaddled the ponies and turned them into the paddock. After eating a huge tea we rushed upstairs and crammed our few belongings into our cases, then hurried down to the yard.

Sara brought out the horse-box and we loaded our tack and cases. Panda was easily caught but Kirsty refused to come near me until I discovered an ancient toffee in my pocket. Even then she tried to snatch it and I only just managed to catch her by the forelock. Sara suggested that her stardom had gone to her head and she was becoming temperamental.

After we had boxed them we leant against the engine, waiting for the trekkers to return so we could say good-bye to them and to Paddy. As we waited we made up idiotic conversations between the screenstruck Kirsty and the cows in her field at home. By the time everyone did arrive we were propped up against the radiator helpless with laughter.

They had had a good day's trekking without any undue excitements. We told them about the film unit and Paddy said we were mad wasting our time on such rubbish when we could have been riding and Geoffrey grumbled that he hadn't been with us. We said good-bye to them all and thanked Paddy for a wonderful week-end. She said she had enjoyed having us and that next time I came I must stay longer and see her Arabs ridden out.

We climbed into the cab of the horse-box, Sara started up the engine and as I leant out of the window waving and trying to catch last glimpses of Chisturn House, she drove away.

As the hedges slipped by we sang at the tops of our voices and gave view-holloas at startled passers-by. I tried to find out from Sara what she thought of my riding but all she would say was that my seat needed strengthening though I rather suspected that her true opinion was worse than that.

Suddenly, as the outskirts of Dunstan came into sight, I realized that I would be back at school tomorrow morning. My heart sank and I longed to be free to spend all my time with ponies. Then I remembered that it couldn't possibly be so very long until the Pony Club gymkhana, and things didn't seem quite so black.

[8]

Sara insisted that I stay for dinner with her. She said that Kirsty could quite easily spend the night there and I could collect her after school on Monday.

We had a wonderful dinner of chicken soup, curried chicken, bamboo shoots and rice followed by pineapple flan. While we had been away Vanity had broken out. Sara's mother had been wakened in the still reaches of Saturday night by the local police force 'phoning to ask her to go at once and remove her horse which was causing havoc in the Manse garden. She said she was petrified of going alone and all Adrian would do was cover his head with the bed clothes and mutter that it couldn't possibly be morning yet. Sara's father grinned into his beard and said nothing.

Apparently the Manse was at the end of a long, dark lane and as Sara's mother couldn't find a torch she went without one. With her heart in her mouth she reached the Manse safely, caught Vanity and apologized to an irate Minister who to her amazement was wearing a night shirt.

Once she started for home she discovered that it was better being alone than being with Vanity who saw bogies in every bush and stood stock still for seconds before any suspicious looking shadow. When she eventually got her home she decided to put her in one of the loose-boxes rather than back into the field from which she had escaped. By the time she had bedded Vanity down and given her a hay net it was a quarter to seven and not worth going back to bed, with the result that she was rather irritable by the evening and not willing to hear a good word about any horse.

We told them all about our week-end and then Sara's father tactfully changed the subject to Daddy's art. Although I know absolutely nothing about art and think the sight of hounds and hunt servants mounted on greys more beautiful than the most famous masterpiece in the world, I have heard Daddy's painting discussed so often I can make more or less intelligent remarks about it. Sara's mother considered his portraits were too modern but her father said they expressed the unrest of our times.

After dinner we went out and said good night to our faithful steeds who were busily employed nibbling each other's necks. Then Sara's father drove me home in their Land Rover.

My family were having one of their enormous supper nights and except for Roland they were all in the kitchen making omelettes. Vixen and Flirt met me with a flurry of wet licks and even Nero condescended to notice me. Everyone listened in a rather abstracted way to my stories. Mummy asked if I had remembered to thank everyone I should have thanked. Daddy said the house was so peaceful without me he was thinking of sending me to boarding school. I stared at him aghast until I realized he was joking.

Stuart said he had missed Kirsty like anything and had calculated that he would have her until a week on Wednesday. I said he could bring her back from Sara's tomorrow night and have her till Sunday. He agreed at once.

'But you can bring her back tomorrow,' he said as he took his omelette through to the study.

I made myself cocoa and waited until Daddy had finished his omelette which was flavoured with a little from every cheese in the house. Mummy's was a very complicated one filled with mushroom pâté so we left her to it and went into the study.

There to my horror sitting with Stuart was Roland and

an unknown girl. My first thought was that Kirsty and I would not have Sara as a pilot for our first hunt. I imagined Kirsty napping and trapping the field in a narrow lane, causing them to miss the run of the season. I saw her refusing fences of two feet and knew the sinking misery of watching hounds and horses disappear from sight which I had known so well when we hunted on foot.

'This is my kid sister Jean,' Roland said. 'You'll need to excuse the dress she lives in. Jean, this is Doreen.'

I scowled at them and muttered, 'How do you do?' I thought Roland's remarks about my clothes quite unnecessary, as she was the worst possible type. Her hair was cut very short and she was wearing black ballet shoes with scarlet ski pants.

'Did you have a good week-end?' Roland asked.

'Ummm,' I said. 'Glorious.'

'What were you doing?' asked Doreen. 'Riding horses all the time?'

'Most of it.'

'Oh, how quaint,' she said and turned to Daddy. 'I was just saying to Roland how much I admire your work. Your portrait of Glyn Howard meant something to me. It gave me a new understanding of his poetry.'

I stopped listening. I had heard it all before. 'Beast,' I whispered to Stuart. 'So that's why you didn't want to bring Kirsty back.'

Stuart grinned, 'You know Sara better than I do,' he said.

'It makes no difference. Roland is mad.'

'There's a letter from the Pony Club. They're having an extra unmounted rally next Friday night. A lecture and a film.'

'What on?'

'Training the young horse. It's to be at the Master's house and guess who's giving it?'

I guessed Pat Smythe and Dorian Williams, but Stuart asked scornfully if we ever did have anyone like that. I said I supposed not and who was it? He said did I remember when we were young and hopeful and went round stables offering our services as tack cleaners and mucker outers going to the Craigton School of Equitation and being turned away by a tall, dark man? I remembered vaguely quarrelling with Stuart about whose turn it was to be spokesman.

'Well it's him,' said Stuart. 'And there's a PS to the letter saying that schedules for the gymkhana will be given out at the rally.'

'Oh, we must go then, even if it means dressing-up and being recognized as unsuccessful tack cleaners.'

'He'll never know us. It was years ago.'

Mummy interrupted Stuart by asking him what we were muttering about and bringing us into the general conversation.

In the morning I was horrified to find my gym tunic still in its brown paper parcel. It was a mass of creases and as I put it on I could hear the voice of my form mistress telling me to see her after school. I covered it with my coat before Mummy saw it but the eagle eye of my form mistress spotted me after prayers and I had to wait until half past four listening to her talking about the honour of the form and my duty to myself to be always smart and tidy.

I decided to collect Kirsty on my way home to cheer myself up after the depressing sight of my form mistress' podgy face. But luck was against me. Sara's house was deserted and when I knocked on the back door a little girl answered. She said a boy had taken the pony away hours ago and added that he looked as if he might have been a horse thief. When I said it would probably be my brother she lost interest and went in to finish her tea.

I hadn't enough money to catch another bus so I walked home swinging my satchel, alternately imagining myself turning into a dressage expert with stables in the Midlands, or growing fat and becoming an office worker who typed all day and watched television every night.

When I reached home Stuart was riding in the field and blithely informed me that he had had a half holiday and changed his mind about collecting Kirsty.

The week dragged slowly on to Friday. Stuart said it was wonderful having Kirsty to himself and I knew it was misery not having her at all. Daddy decided to paint my portrait with my hard hat on, which meant sitting for hours in his studio and inventing plausible excuses at school for undone homework.

The Master, Mr Osborne, lives about a mile away from us and as the rally was at six-thirty we left at six, hoping to arrive in good time. Unfortunately we wasted time talking to Kirsty and had to run most of the way there. In the drive we met Celia and John Dunne who have a Shetland and an ancient hunter. Neither of them are very keen on riding because they are both so desperately afraid of being kicked or bitten. They looked as if they had been quarrelling and seemed pleased to see us.

'Hiya,' Celia called. 'We've been waiting here for hours but John is such a coward he won't knock on the door.'

'We're far too late to go in now,' muttered John. 'And if you think I'm going in now and disturbing everyone you're wrong.'

'We can't be so very late,' Stuart said. 'It's only half past six,' he added looking at his watch.

'It's twenty-to,' answered John. 'Your rotten old watch must have stopped. I'm going home anyway. There's a pop show on television and if I hurry I'll see it.'

'Oh John, you can't go home,' wailed Celia but John was already running down the drive. 'The little beast! Just wait till I get him. Come on, you two, if you're coming. There's no point in standing here.' Turning on her heel she marched up to the front door and rang the bell. We waited a second, then Celia rang again.

We heard the flip-flop of someone in slippers coming to open the door. Somehow when the door opened Celia and Stuart seemed to fade into the background and the old lady's irritable remarks about the youth of today who were always late and then too impatient to wait a minute seemed to be addressed to me alone.

'I suppose you've come to the meeting,' she said. 'You are a quarter of an hour late, but wipe your feet and close the door behind you and we'll see if there are three chairs left.'

She led us, her slippers flapping, through a long passage hung with foxes' masks and brushes, hunting crops and a very old pink coat faded by wind and rain to a wonderful mulberry shade.

'She's the Master's mother,' whispered Celia and Stuart's 'Blimey!' made the old lady turn round and give him a sharp-eyed glare.

She opened a door and we followed her in. The room was in darkness but after we had stood for a few minutes in total blindness we managed to make out four empty chairs at what seemed to be the back of several rows. Thankfully we groped our way to them, sat down, and watched the film which was in progress.

Three men were saddling a bay horse of about fifteen hands. 'Forty years ago the young horse was broken-in and broken in spirit. Today his master is his friend who gently teaches the horse all he wishes him to learn.' The horse on the screen obligingly nuzzled the pocket of the man at his head while the other man slowly tightened the girths. The film dealt with the complete education of the horse from a green youngster to the well-schooled hunter. We saw him at his first hunt and winning at hunter trials.

The film whirled to a close and someone switched the lights on. A tall, lean man stood up and immediately I recognized him as the Craigton riding master and re-membered our visit to his stables quite clearly. He said he hoped we had all enjoyed the film and learnt something from it. He informed us that there was to be an interval for refreshments now and, while he did not wish to keep us from the cakes that Mrs Osborne had so kindly pro-vided, he would like to point out that his lecture which was to follow would not take the usual form but he would do his best to answer one question on horses and horsemanship from each person present. And perhaps while we were gorging ourselves we would give a little thought to our questions just to prove that we possessed the fundamental qualification for anyone aspiring to horsemanship – an inquiring mind.

He sat down and the greedier members made a wild dive for a table at the back of the room which was laden with cakes and brilliantly coloured lemonades. A fat boy sitting next to Celia said he was going to ask why everyone today was so crazy about dressage when his father had been leading the hunting field for years on horses that had never heard the word and would consider you mad if they started riding them in circles or serpentines.

'Come on,' Stuart said, 'there'll be no cakes left if we don't join the scrum now.' Once we were away from the fat boy he added that he remembered seeing him crash his way through a whole set of show jumps on a stargazing grey, and that he was just the type who wrote letters to *Horse and Hound* on the folly of dressage, signing himself Col. Blimp.

As usual I couldn't think of a question to ask, although I only need to be alone with a horse for a minute for my abysmal ignorance to shock me to the core. As we drank our glasses of lemonade and ate iced cakes Stuart said he would ask how soon you could put a young horse into a double bridle and Celia said she would ask how you could avoid being bitten by your horse.

'That sounds more like evidence of fear to me than an inquiring mind,' I said.

'Well you can't think of anything to ask,' replied Celia scornfully. 'That's evidence of an utter blank.'

'I'll think of something, don't worry,' I said.

'Don't worry, I'm not worrying,' Celia said.

'What's all this worrying about?' said a voice behind me and there was our MFH.

'Just girls,' said Stuart in disgusted tones.

'I was wondering if I'd be seeing you out next season on the black pony you've bought?'

'We're hoping to,' I answered.

'We haven't started jumping her yet,' said Stuart.

'Looks to me as if she would have plenty of pop. Usually do these native ponies. What they can't jump over they can jump through. I'd a Dartmoor when I was a boy. She knew the country as well as I did. Darnedest little skirter you ever saw. She would keep you in sight of hounds when hundred pound hunters were fighting their way out of bogs. But that wasn't yesterday. Enjoying the rally?'

We all said we were and thanked Mr Osborne for his hospitality.

'Grand fellow, Captain Valeur. Don't hold with all his ideas myself but he seems to get the results.'

The Master walked away and we went back to our seats. Everyone was talking at once and the noise was terrific. Stuart remarked with a grin that we all had voices that would carry on the hunting field.

The riding master whom we now knew as Captain Valeur stood up and walked to the front of the room and I realized in a panic that I still hadn't thought of a question.

'Shut up at the back there!' he shouted and everyone laughed. 'I shall begin at the front and work my way back. Will you all ask your questions in loud, clear voices so that everyone can hear? Right; first question please.'

Everyone had a question to ask; how to stop a pony getting too fat on rich grazing; how to stop a pony pulling; should a horse that lives out have its legs clipped; how to tell a horse's age from its teeth and many others. The Captain answered them all expertly making quite sure each person understood their answer.

Suddenly I realized that he had reached our row. There was the anti-dressage boy, Stuart, Celia and then myself. I hardly heard his rating down of the anti-dressage boy and I didn't hear any of his rather complicated reply to Stuart about double bridles and the danger of over-flexion. He told Celia that the only sure way of avoiding a horse's teeth was never to go near a horse, but if a horse was a persistent nipper the best cure was to push his head away every time he tried to bite.

Every question I thought of someone had asked already. 'And now for the last question,' Captain Valeur said.

I stood up without the faintest idea of what I was going to ask. On the wall behind Captain Valeur was a portrait in oils of a very grand little lord with a hawk on his wrist riding a dapple grey pony. The pony looked cross and in great need of an understanding pat on the neck.

'If you were a horse,' I asked and the more easily amused members giggled, 'what qualities would you hope for in your rider?'

'A very suitable question to finish up on,' began Captain Valeur. 'What qualities? Patience first, then courage, then consideration. Patience to take a thing slowly until I understood what was expected from me. Courage to give me courage so that I approached every jump with the knowledge that my rider had no doubts about getting to the other side, and consideration when I was tired or just not feeling too good. Consideration that put me before theatres, dances or books no matter how tempting or how bad the weather. And, I think, horse knowledge too. Well-meaning ignorance is just as disastrous as any other kind.'

When Captain Valeur had answered me, Miss Knuttal stood up and gave a vote of thanks. She told us the gymkhana would be in a month's time and as usual it would be part of the Dunstan Agricultural Show and that schedules would be available at the door as we went out. There were rounds of applause for Captain Valeur and Mr Osborne, then everybody started to go home.

'Let's see the schedule,' demanded Stuart when we got outside.

'It's bound to be exactly the same as usual,' moaned Celia. 'There are always more carthorses than anything else. That's the trouble with having it tagged on to an agricultural show.'

'Look Jean,' said Stuart, 'there's a showing class for mountain and moorland ponies.'

'Ridden or in hand?' I asked.

'It's always ridden,' Celia replied. 'It's frightfully select. Not just the Pony Club. Quite famous breeders bring Fell ponies up, and last year there were two Welsh ponies and one of them was first.'

I couldn't remember a thing about it and wondered how it was possible for anyone to go through life being so unobservant.

'You're not thinking of entering that black animal of yours,' exclaimed Celia. 'Why, I wouldn't dream of entering Midget.'

'You might get bitten in the ring and then what would happen?' I asked spitefully.

'Oh, not again!' said Stuart. 'We might enter Kirsty. Why not?'

'You wouldn't stand a chance. It would just be throwing your money away. You'd be far better to save it and spend it on riding lessons,' and with a wave of her hand Celia turned in at her gate.

'She is the utter end,' groaned Stuart. 'No wonder John would rather watch TV.'

'We would need a double bridle to show Kirsty in, wouldn't we?' I asked.

'From what Captain Valeur said she should be all right in one now. It's just if they are rushed into it and the curb is needed to control them that they go all wrong.'

'We haven't got a double bridle,' I pointed out.

'Sara?' inquired Stuart.

'I shouldn't think so, not after Doreen.'

'And we must enter the Pony Club jumping. If we start tomorrow we should manage it,' said Stuart, his ambitions soaring.

'Where are we going to get a double bridle from?' I repeated. 'And come to that, the entrance money?'

'Oh don't worry; we'll manage. Something will turn up.'

'Micawber,' I said.

'Well, it always does,' replied Stuart.

And as I walked home I imagined Kirsty, small and shining and self-possessed, leading round Dunstan show ring with a red rosette in her bridle.

[9]

ABSOLUTELY amazingly, something turned up on Monday morning.

It had been a miserable weekend. The rain had poured down all day on Saturday and Stuart had returned from his ride soaked to the skin. Mummy said she couldn't imagine why anyone wanted to ride in weather like that and Stuart had indignantly pointed out that it was *his* turn for Kirsty that was slipping away while he sat in the house watching the rain, and he was quite sure Mummy had never shared a pony with anyone or she would know how annoying it was to keep getting on and off all the time.

Sunday morning was just as wet and in the afternoon, when it showed signs of brightening up, we were all packed off to visit an old friend of Mummy's who has two of the most feeble children in the world. Their names are Egbert and Jerry Downie and although one is nine and the other nearly eleven they never go anywhere without either their mother or their father. They are perpetually afraid of catching some infectious disease and their favourite topic of conversation is the dreadful illnesses they have survived.

Stuart said he would ride Kirsty on Monday morning before school to make up for the wet weekend. So when I heard him clumping downstairs at five in the morning I turned over and went to sleep again. Mummy said she called me but I must have been too far under the bedclothes to hear her and I slept on until eight o'clock. As my bus goes at a quarter past eight I had a terrific rush and pushed the letter which Roland handed to me into my pocket and proceeded to forget all about it until I was on the bus coming home.

I was sitting next to Anne Chisholm who, although not horsey, is good fun, when I remembered the letter. I dragged it out of my pocket and tried to uncrumple it. The address was typed and I had no idea who it was from.

'Well, open it,' Anne said.

'I don't know anyone who even has a typewriter,' I said as I opened it. 'Perhaps someone has an aged polo pony they want to give away.'

Inside was a typewritten note which read, 'Enclosed please find payment for services rendered,' an an undecipherable signature. Written underneath was 'Buy your cute pony a great big apple. She deserves it. The shots were swell.'

'What is it?' demanded Anne. 'There's something else in the envelope,' and she took it from me. Crimes! it's a cheque for twelve pounds from the Magnate Film Company. Don't tell me you're a film star when you're not at school.'

I couldn't believe my ears. Twelve pounds completely out of the blue!

'Now we can buy a double bridle and have a riding lesson each,' I shouted. 'Oh, Anne, look at it,' and I waved the pink piece of paper in the air, almost knocking off the man's hat who was sitting in front of us. He turned round scowling and muttered that it was lessons in voice control I needed, not in riding.

When I told Stuart the good news he was pleased about the double bridle and about having money for the gymkhana entries but not about the riding lessons. He said it was stupid taking so much notice of Celia's remark. I said it wasn't anything to do with Celia and that we could both do with a lesson.

'What good would the lesson do anyway?' he asked.

I said that as we had hardly done any jumping in our

lives before and were proposing to jump a green pony it might just come in useful.

'We'll buy the bridle first and pay our entry money and see how much is left.'

'I never thought of doing anything else,' I replied. I felt annoyed with him for not being more excited over our good fortune.

I went to look for someone else to tell but could only find Daddy. He said that he had expected that I would get something but not as much as twelve pounds, but those American film companies had money to burn and the world today was losing all sense of value. He then produced my hunting cap from behind some canvases and said he had a few finishing touches to put to my portrait and had I a few minutes to sit for him.

After I had sat for half an hour I suggested that the light was failing and I was hungry. In another half hour Mummy called to say that dinner was ready and I escaped.

When I had finished my homework I took the halter down to the field and gave Kirsty a lesson in trotting in hand. She was inclined to stop suddenly and dig her toes in. I broke a long, springy stick from the hedge and used it with my left hand behind my back. After twenty minutes she was showing signs of improvement and I decided she had had enough for one night.

I left her and walked home. I was sure I was right about the riding lessons. All the books I had read insisted that there was no substitute for lessons from a good instructor. As I was putting my bike away in the shed I discovered Stuart knocking nails into wood.

'Look,' he said, 'cavelettis.' He had nailed two pieces of wood together crossways. 'One way it's four inches, the other six,' he said demonstrating. He had made eight, which gave us four cavelettis.

'It's too late tonight,' I said regretfully.

'I know, idiot. They're for tomorrow. I thought we could

use the clothes poles over them. They won't be very solid but I can't think of anything else.'

'What about the old clothes posts? They would be solider. She would snap the poles if she touched them.'

We found the posts lying on the ground by the wall. Months ago one of them had rotted through and we had had them all replaced by metal ones set in concrete and, as seems to happen rather often in our family, they had just been left lying close to where they had stood.

We dragged them up to the shed. 'Ugh,' I exclaimed as a huge spider ran over my hand. 'I shall keep feeling creepy things all night now.'

We set the posts up on Stuart's stands and ran over them a few times ourselves.

'They would look much nicer painted,' I said. 'If Celia saw them she would say they just suited Kirsty.'

'How many times do I have to tell you that I don't care what Celia or John or Sara or anyone else thinks? Do you realize that the gymkhana is in just over three weeks' time and she will have to be jumping four feet by then?'

'We had better wait until tomorrow night to fill in the entry forms,' I said gloomily, and I went to bed to dream of jumping Kirsty over enormous banks only to find myself stuck on top of them surrounded by furious riding masters. They clamoured for money and threatened to turn Kirsty into a black spaniel unless I allowed them to teach me to ride.

All next day I was haunted by despair. I imagined Kirsty bucking madly at the sight of a pole on the ground. I couldn't think why we hadn't started her jumping education weeks ago. Ann told everyone in our form about the twelve pounds and by four o'clock I was very tired of telling people I was going to buy a double bridle and listening to them laugh scornfully or tap their heads significantly.

I hurried home to find Stuart in his jodhs. sitting on the kitchen table with a mug of coffee in one hand and a cheese sandwich in the other.

'Buck up and change,' he said. 'I've made coffee so we don't need to worry about rushing home to dinner.'

As I changed I told myself that it would not alter the fate of nations if Kirsty refused to jump.

I decided to have black coffee, hoping it would clear my usually vague senses and enable me to apply the correct aids at exactly the right moment. Leaning against the Aga I said conversationally, 'All ponies jump.'

'Not three and a half feet with us on their backs,' said Stuart.

'The Master said she looked as if she had plenty of pop.'

'He was only making polite conversation. Probably he has only seen her outlined on the horizon.'

Gloom descended and we washed up our mugs in silence. Roland came in and asked if we were thinking of going to a funeral.

'Yes,' I replied, 'the funeral of our show jumping hopes.'

'I would give the whole thing up if I were you,' he said cheerfully.

We piled the cavalettis on to the wheelbarrow and balanced the saddle on top. Stuart pushed it and I walked behind carrying the bridle, halter and dandy brush. We were half-way there when the barrow caught on a stone and overturned. Everything fell out and Stuart said several words he is not supposed to use. I painstakingly put everything down and helped him to reload. When we reached the field I discovered I had left the dandy brush behind and I had to go back and collect it.

'Oh come on,' Stuart shouted as soon as he saw me. 'You've been ages.'

'Couldn't find it,' I yelled back.

He haltered Kirsty and tied her to the gatepost. 'If you take the worst of the mud off and saddle her I'll take the cavalettis down to the bottom of the field,' he said.

'O.K.,' I said and started to brush over Kirsty. She was curious about what Stuart was doing. When I untied her to put on her bridle she swivelled round on my foot in her efforts to see him. I tightened the girths and tried to mount while Kirsty twirled around. At last I was up and she bounced down the field while I fumbled with my leathers endeavouring to shorten them, since Stuart had ridden last.

'What on earth are you doing?' Stuart asked when I reached him. 'You look as if you've never been on a horse in your life before.'

'I'm altering my stirrups,' I said with as much dignity as I could muster, 'while using my legs to halt my horse.'

'We'll have half an hour each. You'd better be first, seeing you're up.'

'I'll school for twenty minutes first,' I said and began riding Kirsty about the field at the walk and trot. She was fresh and kept shying at dangerous-looking stones and lurking dandelions. After about ten minutes she was more relaxed and began to pay proper attention to my aids. I took her into my schooling corner and circled her at the trot. As long as I concentrated on my riding and used my legs, she stayed reasonably supple on the bit and with her neck curved inwards, but if I let my mind wander to other things my legs seemed to slip forward and Kirsty stiffened up and circled with her head poking out of the circle. I walked her round twice on a loose rein to let her stretch her neck, then cantered her round three times on each rein.

Stuart, who had been fussing round with the jumps, looked at his watch and told me I had only ten minutes left.

'Right,' I replied, 'we'll start. Hold your thumbs.'

I began by walking her over one pole on the ground and then trotting her over it. She made no fuss whatsoever but trotted calmly and stayed on the bit. My heart rose.

'I'll try four poles on the ground,' I said to Stuart. He laid them out and I trotted her over them several times.

'You've had your time,' Stuart told me.

'I must try her over the pole four inches high,' I

begged. 'Please, Stuart.' Stuart obligingly set up one of the poles and announced, 'Miss Jean Donaldson on Kirsty.'

I circled Kirsty, then trotted her at the pole. As we approached she quickened her steps, I pulled too hard on the reins to bring her back into hand, she stuck her nose in the air and cat-jumped with easily a foot to spare. I lost my seat and sprawled over her neck.

'Terrible!' shouted Stuart. 'You were hanging on her mouth like a load of bricks. Use your legs more and lighter with your hands.'

I took her back and tried again. By using my legs more I managed to keep her straight at the pole but she still cat-jumped and I landed on her neck once more.

'That was a bit better,' encouraged Stuart. 'You can have one more go and then it really is my turn.'

My last attempt was more successful. I managed to keep my seat but only by riding rather wildly and giving Kirsty her head.

I dismounted and gave the reins to Stuart who mounted and took Kirsty over the poles on the ground. She trotted over them smoothly and unconcernedly. Then he took her over the poles six inches high. On his fourth attempt he had her moving well and she trotted over them without altering her stride in any way.

'Oh well done! Jolly good!' I shouted.

He brought her back again and she repeated her performance. We both petted her and fed her titbits from our jodh. pockets, which she condescended to accept.

'I should think that's enough for her first go,' said Stuart. 'She's done rather well. I wonder if she's jumped before.'

'Perhaps. You haven't really had your full time,' I replied.

'I'll survive,' Stuart said and he walked Kirsty to the gate to unsaddle her. As I piled the posts up by the hedge I decided that Stuart was a far better rider than I was and perhaps he didn't need a lesson. I imagined him in ten years time jumping for Britain while I pottered round the countryside on an aged and sedate Kirsty.

That evening we filled in our entry forms for the gymkhana. After a lot of tossing-up and arguing we decided that I should show Kirsty, and Stuart jump her and that we would be strong minded and not enter her for the bending and the potato and bucket race for which, we both knew, she wasn't ready. The entrance was a pound for the jumping and two pounds fifty for the showing class.

Stuart had loads of Latin homework so I went to post the letter and took Flirt and Vixen with me to the pillar box. As I dropped it in I heard it fall with a gentle flop amongst the other letters.

'Do you realize, Vixen,' I said, 'this is the beginning of a new phase in my life. I, Jean Donaldson, am entering for a gymkhana for the very first time.' Vixen listened with her head on one side, then losing interest chased Flirt. I walked slowly homewards through the dusking evening, scuffling through the dusty grass of the roadside and throwing sticks for the dogs.

Next morning I hacked Kirsty before school and at night Stuart trotted her over the cavalettis. She knew what we wanted now and took them calmly without getting behind her bit or cat-jumping.

We hacked and jumped her on alternate days for the rest of the week and by Saturday she was jumping a foot high and a spread of three feet. We were both certain she had jumped before we owned her, but decided not to jump her on Sunday just to make quite sure we were not boring her.

'If she goes stale on us we've had it,' Stuart said, still clinging pessimistically to the gloomiest idea he could find.

On Saturday afternoon we visited the saddlers. Roland was doing nothing so he came too. After a great deal of humming and hawing Mr Duncan disappeared into his back room and reappeared with a second-hand double bridle. He said he had picked it up at a sale of one of the big estates down Drymnton way. He laid it out on the counter and looked at it lovingly. Stuart and I stared at it with suitable admiration but Roland had lost interest and was poking around in the darker corners of the shop. This seemed to distract Mr Duncan's attention for he only spent ten minutes relating the awful instances of un-horsiness that he had come across recently. Then he said, 'I'll let you have it for five pounds and cheap at the price.'

The leather was in good condition and the snaffle nice and broad. 'All right,' I said, 'though I can tell you why so many people stop riding.' And I struggled to pull the money out of my jodhs. pocket.

Mr Duncan looked hurt and said you didn't need to ride with a double bridle. He took my money and offered to wrap up the bridle. I said thank you very much but I could easily manage it. We all said good-bye and trooped out making the bell jangle behind us.

'Now you look as if you'd lost your horse,' said Roland. 'Before you only looked as if you were coming or going from a horse.'

'Let's go and have afternoon tea at that place with the marzipan cakes,' suggested Stuart. 'I'll pay.'

So we all went and sat at the crushed, little tables of the Miss Muffet tea rooms. The waitress looked suspiciously at our jodhs. and Roland's worn corduroys but decided we were harmless and brought our tea and cakes.

Stuart remarked that he had seen the film of *Richard III* with his form on Friday. After Roland had talked Shakespeare for ten minutes Stuart asked me what my favourite film was.

'*My Friend Flicka*,' I answered in surprise for I was quite sure Stuart knew, having been to see it with me three times already.

'Really,' he said. 'It's on at the Regal today. I noticed it when we were passing.'

There was a pause in the conversation and then Roland

went on talking Shakespeare. When Stuart paid the bill, Roland sportingly took the hint and gave us a pound with which to see *My Friend Flicka*, telling us that much as he had enjoyed it the first three times he didn't really want to see it again.

'This will be my eighth time,' I whispered joyfully to Stuart, as we sank back in our seats, 'and I should think we're early enough to see it twice.'

Next morning we hacked Kirsty. It was lovely riding through the deserted Sunday morning lanes with only the sound of her hooves and the birds' song from the hedgerows. She was in one of her most obliging moods and with her ears pricked she trotted on tirelessly. When it was Stuart's turn to ride, I looked at the green fields which stretched away on either side and I wondered if, when Autumn came, I would be galloping over them with the sound of the horn and the music of hounds making my heart beat high with excitement.

In the afternoon we made five jumps in one corner of the field and after an hour and a half of hard labour we sank back exhausted.

'To think,' said Stuart, 'some people do this kind of thing every day for a living.'

'I'd rather be dead,' I agreed.

Our jumps were rather amateurish but looked quite nice. First there was one of the cavalettis at six inches and then a pole on oil cans with poles at the take-off and landing giving it breadth. These were followed by a log and a strange arrangement of brushwood made by Stuart, and then in the middle a post on two old kitchen chairs which we were going to cover with a rug to give it an unusual appearance.

On Monday night we jumped Kirsty round the course for the first time. But something seemed to go wrong. After she had been round once she refused to trot and would only go at a full out gallop, cat-jumping and crashing her way through everything. Stuart was no more successful than I was and we were forced to go back to trotting over cavalettis. She stretched her neck and stayed on the bit, but when Stuart tried her over the twelve inch pole again she refused twice and eventually went over knocking it down after some rather rough riding on Stuart's part.

'I'd better finish on cavalettis work just to leave a good impression,' he said. We were both bitterly disappointed. We had thought she was quite ready for our course and now our jumps were in ruins and would have to be rebuilt.

Somewhere we had gone wrong and things got worse until they reached a climax the following Saturday. I had fallen off twice and been bucked off once and was sitting on the grass trying, rather hazily, to keep Stuart in focus as he took her round.

By the time she had reached the third jump she was galloping full speed and was completely out of control. As Stuart turned her in for the last jump she snatched the reins from his hands and gave a huge leap clearing it with easily two feet to spare. Stuart was not expecting this and sailed over her head but managed to hold on to the reins.

'It's hopeless,' he said as he scrambled to his feet and remounted. 'I'll school her for ten minutes and that will be quite enough for today.'

He worked hard and at the end of ten minutes she was on the bit and moving well.

'It's our jumping,' I said despondently as we led her up the field.

'She cleared easily three feet that last jump,' Stuart said. 'She would have terrific scope if she would only be sensible.'

The sun had been in our eyes as we walked up the field and it wasn't until we had almost reached the gate that we saw Mummy standing at it. She had walked down with Vixen bringing some scraps for Kirsty.

'How much do you think she saw?' muttered Stuart.

Our worst fears were confirmed when she greeted us

and said, 'You seem to be having a bit of trouble with your jumping. My heart has been in my mouth all the time I've been watching you. Have you finished for to-night?'

We assured her we had and she patted Kirsty and fed her the scraps she had brought down.

'She's looking very well. You must have spent ages on her with a body brush, Jean.'

'Well, not really ages,' I replied. 'But she is looking well and she is going awfully well in the double bridle.' I was determined to bring all the good points well to the fore.

'Don't rush, but tea is ready when you are,' and Mummy called Vixen who was rabbiting in the hedge-rows and walked back home.

'She couldn't possibly have seen everything,' said Stuart, 'or she would have made much more fuss. The second time you came off it rather looked as if you were going to be mixed up with Kirsty's feet but somehow she missed you.'

'If she'd seen that I'm sure she would have stopped us. Maybe she only saw you and really you looked quite con-trolled.'

But our optimism was short lived. As soon as we sat down to tea Daddy remarked, 'I'd no idea you were still falling off horses. I thought you were past that stage by now.'

I said, 'Did you know I found that sheepskin mitten I lost. It was in my bicycle bag.'

And Stuart said, 'Flirt woke me up in the middle of the night last night to show me a mouse she must have caught days ago.'

Unfortunately we both spoke at once so our clumsy efforts to distract Daddy's attention were wasted.

'Don't try and change the subject,' he said. 'That's only a confession of guilt. I don't mind you falling off now and again but from your mother's account of your afternoon's activities it's a wonder you both haven't got broken backs.'

'I only came off once,' said Stuart indignantly. 'And if I'd known she was going to jump as high as she did, I wouldn't have come off even then.'

'Jean fell off three times,' said Mummy, 'and the second time I was sure she was going to be trampled on. You can't possibly go on the way you are doing.'

'But we absolutely must,' I almost shouted, feeling like a swimmer struggling against immense waves. 'It's the gymkhana a week on Saturday and she's entered for the jumping.'

'My dear daughter,' said Daddy, 'I value your neck far more than any rosette you may win on Saturday.'

'And anyway,' added Mummy, 'the idea of entering Kirsty for any gymkhana jumping the way she is just now, is quite out of the question. It must be very bad for a young pony to go on knocking down jumps and I should hate to watch you giving an exhibition like today's in public.'

I knew that Mummy was right but I knew equally certainly that we couldn't give in.

'We can't possibly scratch,' I said. 'We must enter for the jumping.' But Daddy had stopped listening to me.

'You're not to jump that pony again until you get advice from somewhere.' His voice allowed no argument. 'You must be able to see for yourselves that something has gone very wrong and there is no use going on making it worse. Gymkhana or no gymkhana, there is to be no more jumping until you get yourselves straightened out.'

I sat in blackest misery. We were utter and complete failures. To scratch from the gymkhana was the end of all my hopes and plans. I heard again the scornful voice of the Leggat girl, 'Of course they scratched at the last minute. I can't imagine why they bought a pony. Their borrowed carthorses were really quite suitable for all they ever do with a horse.'

Stuart had hardly said a word and yet it was worse for him because he had been going to ride her. He was sitting dourly staring into space and looked so utterly miserable I tried again.

'Perhaps if we only jumped her over two jumps . . .'

'Jean,' Daddy said. 'I've told you you are not to jump that pony again until you get help from somewhere, and I don't want to hear any more about it.'

[10]

I was wakened in the still reaches of the night by a dog licking my face. I switched on my bedside light and discovered Flirt, grinning all over her face in the special way spaniels can. I pushed her down before she really got started on my left ear.

'You little wretch,' I told her. 'Go to your box at once. Oh, you are a bad little dog!'

She looked rather crestfallen but trotted off. I lay and listened to the rattle of her claws on the linoleum and her bumping her way downstairs.

Suddenly I remembered the tragedy that had befallen us last night and I wished with all my heart Flirt hadn't wakened me to the cruel realities of life. After tea I had made mad suggestions to Stuart, such as jumping Kirsty miles away from home and then astounding our family with our polished performance at the gymkhana, or giving up our beliefs in the balanced seat and schooling her sitting well back in the saddle and kicking her into the jumps with a few whacks from our crops to help her on. Stuart was horrified and said he could only hope the shock had been too much for me and that I hadn't meant a word I'd said. Then I heard Flirt coming back.

'Bad dog,' I shouted as loudly as I dared. 'Go back to your box.' But she continued to bustle along the landing quite unperturbed. I didn't want to wake everyone up, so I sat up in bed and waited for her. She eased her way through my door and wriggling and bowing she laid a very dead mouse by my bed. When Flirt catches something she hides it and then appears in the middle of the night with her trophy expecting to be praised. Unless it is taken from her she hides it again and reappears with it the next night.

'Oh, you misery,' I said. 'Is that the same one as you had last night?'

She grinned and turned the mouse remains over with her nose. Very reluctantly I got out of bed and picked it up by the tail. Holding it well in front of me I took it downstairs and dropped it into the Aga. I put Flirt back to her box, closed the kitchen door firmly behind me and crept back upstairs.

When I reached Stuart's door it opened and his tousled head appeared.

'I've been thinking,' he said. 'You'd better come in for a minute.'

'It's frightfully late,' I muttered as I sat down on his bed and pulled the eiderdown round my shoulders. 'Would you like to be as quick as you possibly can? It seems hours since Flirt woke me up.'

But now Stuart had got me installed as a rather unwilling audience he seemed in no hurry to reach the point

but rambled on giving a very depressing account of our prospects for the gymkhana. In spite of my efforts I couldn't keep my eyes open. I was almost asleep when I realized that Stuart had stopped talking. I struggled back to consciousness to hear him say in irritated tones, 'Don't tell me you're asleep?'

'Of course not,' I replied. 'I think you're quite right; absolutely right – in fact, I couldn't agree with you more.'

Stuart looked pleased. 'I know it is rather clutching at straws but I've racked my brains for hours and it's the only solution I can think of. We'll 'phone first thing in the morning.'

'Yes, definitely,' I agreed, wondering how I was ever going to discover what we were talking about.

'And you do think Captain Valeur's is the best place?'

'Oh yes,' I said and suddenly realized Stuart was suggesting riding lessons. 'But you were so against it when I suggested them,' I exclaimed in amazement.

Stuart had obviously been expecting this since the beginning and said in defensive tones, 'Well, I've changed my mind and that's that.'

'It's our only chance,' I added as I wandered back to bed.

Just before I fell asleep I thought of the scathing comments Captain Valeur was bound to make about my riding. I wanted to go back and tell Stuart that it would be best if he had two riding lessons and I stayed at home but I was asleep before I could get myself out of bed again.

Immediately after breakfast Stuart brought the telephone directory from the study and looked up the number. He had not agreed to my idea that he should go alone but said that with two people there was a better chance of us remembering Captain Valeur's advice correctly. He found the number and said I could 'phone. I said it was quite all right, *he* could 'phone.

'Well if you don't want to we'd better toss for it,' and he dug in his pocket for a coin.

'Heads,' I shouted as the penny twisted in the air.

'Tails it is,' said Stuart. 'You 'phone. It's Dunstan 237.'

'But what shall I say?' I asked, but Stuart was already dialling.

'Don't be so feeble,' he said. 'Just explain the situation and say we would like riding lessons. How many will depend on how much he charges. There, it's ringing now.' And he handed the receiver to me.

I heard a click and a voice said: 'Hello, Craighton School of Equitation.'

'Hello,' I said. 'I should like to inquire about riding lessons.'

'Yes,' said the voice and waited.

There was a deadly silence while I racked my brain for the right thing to say.

'Hello, hello,' said the voice anxiously. 'Are you still there?'

'For goodness' sake get a move on, Jean,' said Stuart.

'It's all right for you,' I said meaning Stuart, but the voice said, 'Pardon, Madame?' in indignant tones.

'Ask how much they charge,' prompted Stuart.

'I was wondering how much you charge,' I said down the receiver.

'Well, it rather depends how many lessons you wish to take and the standard required. Captain Valeur has a course of seven lessons for beginners which costs five pounds. Or were you wanting something more advanced?'

'Go on, explain,' said Stuart.

'Well, actually, I think we will only be able to afford one lesson each. You see it's like this . . .' And I started to explain about our parents' ban on jumping Kirsty and about the gymkhana being so soon.

Half-way through my explanation the voice said: 'Excuse me. I think it would be better if you spoke to Captain Valeur himself. Just hold the line a minute.'

'She has gone to get Captain Valeur,' I told Stuart. As

I listened I heard the Captain's brisk footsteps approaching. He picked up the phone and said, 'Good morning, Captain Valeur here. To whom am I speaking?'

'Jean Donaldson here,' I said.

'Ah yes,' he replied. 'Having a bit of bother with that black pony of yours. Not overfacing her, are you?'

'I shouldn't think so. None of the jumps were much more than eighteen inches high.'

'Oh, she should manage those. Well if you like to come for a lesson I'll see if I can help you. One hour's instruction is one pound fifty.'

'There's my brother as well,' I said, 'so I'm afraid we will only manage one lesson each.'

'Just as you like,' said the Captain. 'What time would suit you?'

'When?' I asked Stuart.

'Sooner the better,' he replied.

'We've entered for the Pony Club jumping,' I told Captain Valeur, 'so we would like to come as soon as you could take us.' After I had said it I thought it sounded decidedly wrong and rather as if Captain Valeur were the dentist, but he didn't seem to notice.

'Actually I have no class from three-thirty to four-thirty today. My assistant instructor takes out a ride but the two girls I normally instruct are on holiday in Davos. Would that time suit you?'

I said it would and we both said good-bye and rang off. Immediately I was seized by the most dreadful needle. I told Stuart the details of the conversation which he hadn't managed to catch despite his breathing down my neck during most of the 'phone call. Mummy came in and we told her that we were going for a riding lesson that afternoon.

'That's fine,' she said. 'Here's hoping he can help you.'

'He's supposed to be first class,' said Stuart. 'He'll probably collapse when he sees us on horseback. How I wish I'd been born into a family where everyone rides from birth.'

'You don't,' I contradicted. 'Just think of those ghastly children who can't hunt without a doting mother there to tighten their girths and continually correct their seats.'

It was a first class subject for an argument but Mummy interrupted us by saying that we had only half an hour till church and she supposed we both had our bedrooms still to tidy.

I could hardly eat any lunch. My needle, which had been growing all through church, had assumed gigantic proportions by lunch time. Roland said he would wash up for us and let us get away. We had decided to cycle to Captain Valeur's because the Sunday buses were few and far between. We reckoned that if we were away by half past two we would have plenty of time in case of accidents or bike breakdowns. At a quarter past two we were ready and dragging our bicycles out of the shed.

'It's strange how horsey people who can't afford a car always seem to go around on the most decrepit bicycles imaginable,' said Stuart.

'It's because they never clean them,' I said, for our ancient bicycles seemed hardly worth bothering about.

I was quite certain I would make an absolute fool of myself. As we pedalled along I imagined myself hopping around unable to mount and the ignominy of a leg up or, worse still, a mounting block being dragged from a corner of the yard where it had lain untouched for years. Captain Valeur would probably have to spend the whole hour teaching me to canter correctly while Stuart waited livid with impatience.

Captain Valeur's stables were at the back of a huge Georgian Mansion which was now taken over by the Ministry of Pensions. Stuart suggested that we should leave our bicycles in the rhododendron shrubbery at the head of the drive. We were discussing the matter when a lady wearing fawn breeches, boots, an immaculately cut riding coat and a bowler, swished past us in a scarlet sports car. We looked at each other and nodded and wheeled our rusty cycles into the depths of the rhododendrons.

'It's almost half past,' said Stuart. 'We don't want to miss any of our one pound fifty's worth.' We both ran down the drive and on down a lane to the stable yard. There were loose-boxes on three sides with a double row on the right-hand side. An old gentleman, who had once given us a lift in his car when we were following hounds on foot, had told us that the double row had originally been used for visiting mares when the premium stallion for the County had stood here. Now the second row seemed to be mostly filled with children's ponies.

A little girl with long plaits and a brown hunting cap was leading a twelve hand black pony from one of the boxes. In the yard the lady who had passed us had exchanged her sports car for a steel grey hunter with a hogged mane and was talking to two men on bay horses. A girl in ratcatcher came out from one of the boxes leading a chestnut thoroughbred. She attached a leading rein to the little girl's pony, saw her safely aboard and mounted herself. She had an air of authority and I decided she must be Captain Valeur's assistant. The lady and the two men gathered up their reins and the ride started off down the lane. As they passed us, the girl in ratcatcher told us that the Captain would be out in a minute.

'I liked the grey,' Stuart said. 'Do you think they ride here every week?'

'They might be their own horses at livery,' I suggested.

There were two horses standing saddled and bridled and held by pillar reins. We walked over and spoke to them. One was dapple grey with rather a Roman nose and black muzzle, mane and tail. The other was a roan of about fifteen hands.

'I should think these are ours,' Stuart said. 'The grey yours and the roan mine.'

I eyed the grey appraisingly but she didn't look so very much higher than Kirsty. 'What do you bet he says we are beyond all hope and refuses to teach us?'

As I spoke Captain Valeur came into the yard. He was

wearing a tweed jacket, boots and buff breeches. We shook hands and introduced ourselves.

'I remember you now,' he said. 'You were both at the last Pony Club rally and you're the boy who asked the question on double bridles. How is your pony going in it? You're not jumping her in it are you?'

'She's going very well in it,' Stuart replied, 'but we've kept her in a snaffle for jumping.'

'Fine, fine,' said Captain Valeur. 'A double is all right for the show ring but not for jumping. A jog in the mouth from the curb at the critical moment has caused more faults than bears thinking about.' He took the pillar reins off the two horses and led them out. 'The grey is yours,' he said handing me the reins. 'His name is Dexter. And Sepia is yours,' he said to Stuart.

I tightened my girths and Dexter stood like a rock while I mounted. Whenever I was up my needle vanished. I patted his hard, grey neck and tried to keep my seat, arms and legs in the correct places.

'We'll go down to the indoor school,' said Captain Valeur and led the way. It was a large school but in spite of this it felt strange to be riding indoors. The Captain stood in the middle and told us to walk our horses round the school.

'Use your legs, Jean,' he said. 'All movements of your legs, seat and hands must be co-ordinated. As you collect your horse with your legs and seat you must feel the collection with your hands. Your legs are too far forward. Even an inch can make a difference in your leg position.'

He told Stuart to keep his hands light and to sit farther forward in the saddle. Then we changed rein and trotted.

'Your legs are still too far forward, Jean,' he said. 'Let your knees absorb more of the action and then you won't have to post so high.'

Next we crossed our stirrups and trotted and cantered without them. Dexter had a beautifully smooth, effortless canter. It felt like flying as he moved with a long, low stride around the school.

'Your legs are going forward, Jean,' the Captain said. 'Keep Dexter going. He's a schooled horse but don't let him take you. You're slipping back, Stuart. Whenever you slip back you're out of balance and you stiffen up in your efforts to stay on.'

After we had cantered round a few times on each rein we put a knot in our reins and holding them lightly with one hand we tried to touch our toes in rhythm with the canter. Our efforts were not very successful and Captain Valeur said we should practise it at home with Kirsty on the lunge. He told us that any stiffness in the rider was felt at once by the horse and created one of the vicious circles so frequent in riding which only the rider could break by constant self criticism.

We were then told to shorten our stirrups and Captain Valeur set up two jumps in the middle of the school. He told us to jump them once, then circle round and jump them again. Stuart jumped first. I waited until he was over both jumps before I rode Dexter after him. We managed to jump clear both times but I was rather closer to Stuart when we finished than when we started.

'Legs, Jean, legs,' said Captain Valeur as he walked over to us. 'I can tell you now why your pony won't jump. As you jump you both stiffen in the saddle. Although you do not quite job your horse's mouth, your wrists and elbows are too rigid to allow the necessary give and your hands are unsympathetic enough to hurt the horse's mouth as he lands. That in itself is quite enough to discourage a green horse. Also you both try to tell your horse when to take off which results in a disunity just when you should be doing nothing to distract your horse's attention from the jump. I know you're both thinking of the show jumping experts who ask their horses to take off and perform acrobatics as they go over the jumps, but they are the experts. Remember always that the method is as good as the man and no better. Now Jean, if you would try again.

Sit still all the time and consciously keep your arms and hands relaxed.'

We all worked hard for the remaining time and by the time our lesson ended I was managing to keep still in the saddle and could feel the difference in Dexter's jumping. Captain Valeur seemed pleased with Stuart's progress. He asked him if he was jumping Kirsty at the gymkhana and when Stuart said he was, Captain Valeur said it would be best if no one but Stuart jumped Kirsty until after the gymkhana.

We led the horses back to the yard, unsaddled them and left them pulling at their hay nets. I produced three very crumpled pound notes from my jodhs. pocket and gave them to Captain Valeur. He thanked us and said if he could be of any more assistance just to let him know.

Meanwhile the ride had returned and the smart lady offered us a lift home in her sports car. She said she had often seen us out with a Highland pony and that she lived quite close to us. There was an awkward pause, then Stuart said, 'Thank you very much but actually we're cycling.' Everyone looked round surreptitiously for our cycles but they were all too polite to mention the fact that they couldn't see them. The two men got into a pale green Armstrong Siddeley and drove away; the little girl was collected by a chauffeur and the smart lady started up her sports car and scorched down the drive. Stuart and I thanked Captain Valeur, said good-bye and went to unearth our cycles from the depths of the rhododendrons.

'I'll jump her before school tomorrow morning,' Stuart said. 'You could come too and move the jumps for me.'

'Course I'll come,' I said. 'Now you come to think of it, you can almost hear Kirsty saying. "The sooner I get this over the better," and making one mad rush through the jumps.'

'Yes,' agreed Stuart. 'I suppose over the cavalettis we weren't hurting her nearly so much and she could just grin and bear it.'

Monday morning's jumping was most successful. I set

up three jumps keeping them low and wide as the Captain had advised. Stuart sat very still and tried desperately to keep his hands as light as possible. Kirsty noticed the difference almost at once and her third time over she was thinking about what she was doing, looking at the jumps and moving at a controlled speed.

The next Friday Mummy came down to watch her and was astonished at the improvement. 'It just shows,' she said, 'how a little help from a professional can straighten things out.'

I agreed with her but said we were quite sure Kirsty had been very well broken-in and had done some jumping before she came to us. I sat on the gate beside Mummy and we watched Stuart jump Kirsty round our course, which still had five jumps but was considerably squashed down. They looked very nice together. Stuart's jumping had improved a lot. He sat very still on Kirsty and she jumped cleanly with tremendous spring in her take-offs. She seemed relaxed and enjoying her jumping and altogether very fit.

On the Thursday night before the gymkhana Stuart jumped her round the course for the last time. The jumps were higher than their original heights but she nearly jumped a clear round, only knocking the pole under the rug on the last jump.

'That's us finished until Saturday,' Stuart said halting beside me. 'I'm sure to let her down dreadfully. I feel it in my bones. It's bad enough doing something daft when there's just yourself, but when you're dragging your pony's reputation through the mire as well, it just doesn't bear thinking about.'

I felt exactly the same. I was sure Kirsty could have gone into the ring and shown herself and come out with a rosette without any trouble but with me there anything might happen. I had planned a simple show in case I should be asked to give one. I would ride a figure of eight at the canter slowing down to a trot in the middle, then rein back, turn on the forehand and back to the line.

Kirsty had become most proficient at standing squarely and trotting in hand, so I was fairly confident that she wouldn't let me down if I were asked to unsaddle her and trot her out.

On Friday night we gave our tack a final clean. It was a grey, hazy evening and as we sat on the shed steps rubbing frantically, all the midges in Tarentshire seemed to be there to gorge themselves on us.

'Tomorrow night everything here will be exactly the same. We will be sitting cleaning tack but the gymkhana will be over,' observed Stuart.

'We will either have redeemed our name in the Pony Club or, if possible, have sunk still lower,' I said.

'Won't it be foul if it pours with rain. Can you remember about four years ago they had to cancel the whole thing because the weather was so bad?'

'It's absolutely unthinkable,' I replied. 'It's funny; I feel all churned up inside at the thought of tomorrow but I wouldn't miss a minute of it for anything.'

'Everything that matters is like that,' Stuart said. 'It's the way people are made. You have to go on going on or you might as well not be here at all.'

When we had finished the leather was gleaming like freshly peeled conkers and the buckles, bits and stirrup irons were shining. The double bridle was the most satisfactory but everything, although sportingly old, looked beautifully clean.

We set our alarms for four o'clock which Roland said was being ridiculous. Stuart said he wished he was superstitious, then he could have carried out all kinds of rituals to bring us luck tomorrow. I replied that our fates were already sealed and went to bed to dream of galloping a milk-white stallion over endless grassy plains.

[11]

OVER the familiar garden lay the bleak chillness of the moments before dawn. I stood at my window staring out at the scene I knew so well. The whole world seemed to be waiting tensed for the first light of the sun without which it could not move forward into the day and I too waited, unwilling to start the day to which I had been looking forward for so long. I knew, once I woke Stuart, the day would avalanche away from me, faster and faster, until I stood here again and the garden beneath me was gentle with the evening.

Somewhere a bird called, testing the silence. Once, and then a second time, more surely, a shrill hammer sending jagged cracks of sound over the night's surface. Miraculously the first light of the sun appeared and the whole garden sighed and stretched, colour came back to the world and I could wait no longer. The day had begun.

I dug Stuart out from under his bedclothes. 'Stuart, wake up. Your alarm must have gone off ages ago. And it's today. The gymkhana.'

Stuart sat up, blinking owlishly in the light. 'You wouldn't think anyone could sleep through Jericho and I put her on a tin plate too,' he said and gave his battered alarm clock an affectionate push. 'I'll be with you in a moment.'

'Right,' I said. 'I'll go and catch her.'

I collected the halter from behind the kitchen door and a big slice of bread from the bread bin. The dogs looked at me without bothering to uncurl themselves, only their tails thumping in welcome.

Outside everything was new and fresh. It was going to

be a perfect day – warm, but with a breeze. I ran down the road to Kirsty's field swinging the halter and feeling the breeze blow back my hair.

Kirsty was grazing but when I called she lifted her head and came slowly but steadily towards me. I walked to meet her through the long grass, the dew soaking the turn-ups of my jeans and pollen from the buttercups staining my legs. I was pleased to see she hadn't been rolling and only her off side was damp from lying down. Her lips were soft against my hand as she took the bread while I slipped the halter on. 'Come on my lass,' I said in hearty tones. 'You've rather a lot to do today.' She pricked her ears and I loved the honest, gentle inquiry in her eyes.

I led her back to the house where Stuart was up and being efficient. He had assembled all our grooming kit by the shed, so I took Kirsty over and tied her up and started to groom. We groomed her between us, washed her tail and put the finishing touches to her mane.

For once in our lives we had plenty of time. After a leisurely breakfast we changed into our riding things. My jodhs. looked strangely light after their visit to the cleaners and my string gloves were an unremembered yellow after Mummy's boiling.

Downstairs Mummy was giving Stuart packets of sandwiches for our lunch. She wished us good luck and said that despite the danger of becoming the doting parents which Stuart and I were always blethering about, she and Daddy were going to come and see Stuart jump. Stuart said all they would see was three refusals but if they thought it was worth paying money to see that there was nothing to stop them coming.

Kirsty was standing dozing in the sunlight. She did look nice but it seemed to be tempting Fate to remark on it so I said nothing.

We saddled and bridled her with her gleaming tack. I dragged out my bike and packed the sandwiches into the basket along with the grooming things, the halter and the double bridle. Stuart mounted and we started off.

Kirsty was filled with the joys of life. She bucketed all over the place, shying and jogging and tossing her head.

'We'd better trot,' Stuart said. 'If she goes on like this she'll be in a muck sweat before we are anywhere near the showground.'

She settled down at the trot, and with her head and tail held high she pranced into Dunstan. About two miles from the show Stuart pulled her to a walk. She had recovered from her morning skittishness and walked out well.

As we topped a rise in the road we saw the show sprawled out before us. The billowing, white tents, the show rings with their bright, white poles and in one corner round-abouts and swing-boats already grinding out their mad, gay music.

'Look,' said Stuart pointing, 'isn't that Sara?'

'Yes,' I answered, 'but it's not Panda she's riding. Must be Vanity.'

We waited for a minute at the top of the hill watching her ride into the show.

'Hi!' yelled a voice behind us, making Kirsty jump into the hedge. It was Celia on her bay hunter. He was looking older and more remotely dignified than ever, despite the fact that Celia had obviously been hurrying him.

'I've been trying to catch you up for miles,' she screamed. 'I was almost ready when you passed my gate but this beast wouldn't let me mount. He kept cow kicking.'

We rode down the hill together. Celia had plaited her hunter's mane but the result was rather unsuccessful and the plaits hung in various stages of disarray.

'John is somewhere behind,' Celia said, then she added that Kirsty looked worn out. Stuart ignored this remark and asked her what she was entering for.

'Oh, the usual,' Celia replied. 'The competitions and musical chairs. Dunblane is frightfully musical so he nearly always manages to keep me in till the reserve stage, anyway.'

Once in the showground we found a quiet corner and then I went to collect our numbers. I was 45 and Stuart was 71. As I walked back to our corner I studied them but could not feel any great attachment to 45.

'Your class is next but one,' Stuart told me. He had changed Kirsty's bridle and was giving her a final polish.

'Do you think we're utterly mad showing her?' I asked him.

'Too late now, even if we are,' he answered rubbing a little vaseline round her nostrils and eyes.

I handed Stuart his number and started to tie mine on. It felt queer on my bare arm but I had known all along that I should have had a jacket in which to show Kirsty. 'Does it look O.K.?' I asked Stuart.

He screwed his eyes up against the sun. 'Bit odd,' he replied. 'But it can't be helped I suppose.'

I was wondering just how odd it would look in the ring when Celia's voice interrupted my thoughts.

'I can't find John and Midgey ...' she stopped in mid sentence. 'Don't tell me you are going to show a pony like that,' she squealed. 'I thought it was a bit strange when you didn't have a jacket on, but then you never do wear one do you?'

'I haven't got one,' I replied.

'Gosh, you are feeble,' she shouted. 'Why didn't you ask me for mine?' and she started to take her jacket off. 'I'd jolly well like to see some of those stuck-up women being put in their places.'

Her jacket fitted me quite well but felt strange in the way other people's clothes always do. It was a greeny Harris tweed and my number looked much better on the sleeve of it. Stuart hadn't said anything and I wondered if his pride was wounded.

'I think I'd better mount and ride her round a bit,' I said. I rode in a circle and practised turns and backing. I was thinking how lucky I was to be me, to be alive and to be riding my own pony, when I saw Stuart waving madly. I cantered over to him.

'It is your class,' he was saying. 'They're shouting your number. What on earth were you dreaming about?'

I hurried Kirsty over to the collecting ring. My stirrups felt different lengths and my hard hat was digging into the back of my neck.

'Number forty-five,' said the steward, ticking me off his list as I joined the others in the class. Halting Kirsty, I looked around me. There were two grey Welsh ponies being ridden by middle-aged ladies who looked like sisters. They both had grey hair tinted blue and were riding their ponies in small circles and talking to each other in loud cultured accents. There were two Fell ponies, one ridden by a red-faced, elderly man and the other by a boy who didn't look much older than myself. The rest of the ponies were all Highlands. One was a silver biscuit roan, three were dun, one with a black eel stripe. The fifth was black and was being ridden by a fat girl in ratcatcher. Everyone else was wearing black riding coats, breeches and boots and I was glad to have her as a companion in poverty.

Her pony refused to stand still. He kept throwing his head and barging his quarters into the ponies next to him. He looked decidedly shaggy and not very well groomed, while his tack was dry and dirty. The awful thought struck me that the professional women on the Welsh ponies would think of me like that. Then the Clydesdale mares and foals came out of the ring and we went in – first the Welsh ponies, then one of the dun Highlands and then myself. Kirsty was peering about her in amazement and paying no attention to my aids. I sat down hard and concentrated on my riding.

The steward gave the order to trot and everyone trotted round except the girl on the unkempt Highland. Her pony was absolutely fed-up with the whole thing and was taking her crabwise out of the ring. Kirsty was showing off and I could feel her stretching herself at the trot.

'Canter on,' called the steward and I eased Kirsty into a canter. She rushed rather to begin with, but I managed to collect her and keep her at a slow canter behind one of the

Fells. Just as I was enjoying the canter we were told to walk again. I pulled Kirsty to a walk and patted her neck. The other girl in ratcatcher had disappeared completely. I felt rather a fraud being left in with the professionals and suddenly I realized that my hands were bare. I was just wondering where I had left my string gloves when I thought I heard the steward calling number forty-five into the centre. I stared straight in front and told myself that I was getting so conceited that I would soon be unbearable.

Kirsty was arching her neck and walking out beautifully. When I passed Stuart I gave him a grin which was meant to convey that Kirsty was going well. Stuart in a very loud whisper told me to get into the centre and I realized that the steward was calling me.

I trotted Kirsty across and the elder judge who was wearing plus fours and had a little, bristling moustache grunted and said, 'Are you deaf?' But the younger judge said the loudspeaker system was defunct and that the wind had been blowing in the wrong direction.

I did my best to make Kirsty stand straight while one Welsh pony, then the old gentleman's Fell, then the other Welsh pony were called in, the other ponies forming the back line.

Then the younger judge asked me if I would give my show. As I rode out from the line I wished that I wasn't first and then I could have watched someone else.

I cantered a figure of eight but she was a little heavy on my hands on our right circle. I halted and backed three steps, then took three steps forward, halted and did a turn on the forehand before I trotted back to the line. The elderly judge thanked me and asked the lady on the Welsh pony to give her show. She, too, cantered a figure eight but something went wrong in the middle and Stuart told me afterwards that the pony was disunited after she had attempted a flying change.

There were more people round the ringside now and I wondered if amongst them there were other children longing for a pony to ride. I remembered our long winter of work and thought how far away it seemed.

'She must be deaf,' said a voice beside me and looking down I saw the elderly judge standing with the red rosette in his hand. 'At last! I thought you were in a trance. That's a very nice little pony you have there. Take her to a few more local shows, then try her at the Highland. I'll be surprised if she doesn't make it worth your while.' Then he handed me the red rosette.

'But that's the red one,' I said trying to give it back to him.

'Judge's decision final,' and he passed down the line while I tried to say thank you. He gave the blue rosette to the Fell and a green to the Welsh pony.

The old man on the Fell said, 'Well done, my girl,' and told me to give them a canter round. It felt like someone else cantering the winning pony round the ring, not in the least like the normal day-dreaming Jean Donaldson. Then Kirsty gave a terrific shy at a child waving a paper streamer and I lost a stirrup and felt like myself again.

I rode back to Stuart and dismounted. 'She was absolutely super,' he kept saying. 'She looked absolutely super.' We offered Kirsty carrots and sugar which she ate with the air of one who has done her best and not been found wanting.

We unsaddled Kirsty, put her halter on and sat on the grass holding her and eating our lunch. The breeze had dropped and the heat seemed to grow greater as the show became more and more crowded. Celia found us and congratulated us. I thanked her and returned her jacket. Then we lay on the grass watching Kirsty graze.

The jumping class was quite a big one as most of the Pony Club members who owned ponies entered. Stuart had saddled Kirsty and was riding her round to loosen her up, when Daddy and Mummy arrived. They were both pleased at Kirsty's earlier triumph but inclined to be amused as well.

The Pony Club jumping was before the open jumping

so at two o'clock we made our way down to the ringside and waited for it to begin. Stuart was jumping ninth. He had become very superior and distant which I knew was an outward sign of the needle. He said the jumps looked child's play and gave a hollow laugh.

There were six jumps but the first five competitors only reached the third jump. Two were carried out by their mounts, two had three refusals and the fifth fell off and lay on the ground until she was carried off by one of the stewards. Five minutes later she was riding round on her pony again and her mother was telling her what a brave little girl she was.

Daddy, who was beginning to get rather bored with this shocking display, kept asking why they entered when their ponies couldn't jump. Luckily a small, fair girl who was next jumped a clear round. She was riding a bay thoroughbred who obviously adored jumping and galloped round the course, loving every minute of it. The two other boys before Stuart got round but they both collected plenty of faults on their way.

Then it was Stuart. He rode into the ring and Kirsty looked smaller and more native ponyish than ever. Although I had had no needle in the morning I suddenly had the most dreadful one for Stuart. My legs felt weak and my hands clammy.

The bell rang and Stuart rode Kirsty at the first jump, a pair of hurdles. She cleared it and cantered on to the brush fence. I held my breath and she was over it as well. Stuart turned her for the next jump, a stile. I sat breathlessly watching while she cleared it, too, and was rushing on to the wall.

I saw her prick her ears and goggle. 'She is going to stop,' I said desperately. She slowed down almost to a stand still and blew over the wall. Against all the rules of equitation Stuart kicked her and used his stick. Kirsty gathered herself on her haunches like a cat. I saw her spring then I shut my eyes in an agony of excitement. I heard the a-a-h-h of the crowd and opened my eyes to see Kirsty

galloping on to the parallel bars and a brick from the top
of the wall lying on the green grass. She sailed over the
parallel bars. Stuart turned her and she took the last jump
– a rather shaky triple – in fine style and Stuart rode out
of the ring at a hand gallop followed by the applause of
the crowd.

Mummy was looking very pleased and Daddy warned
her against doting and said that they must accept it as if it
were an everyday occurrence in case any of my horsey
friends were listening. Stuart rode up and dismounted. We
all patted Kirsty and fed her titbits. The loudspeaker announced that competitor 71 had had four faults.

'It was all my fault,' Stuart said. 'I hadn't her properly
collected as we were coming up to the stile and she just
got away from me once we were over it. I thought she was
going to stop altogether.'

Daddy said it had had great audience appeal and
Mummy was unsporting enough to suggest that Stuart
might be second. Stuart said that there were bound to be
dozens more clear rounds and the main thing was that
Kirsty had improved.

Then to everyone's astonishment Ronald and Sara, leading Vanity, appeared. They were both laughing and looked as if Doreen had never existed. Sara congratulated us and said that Stuart had put up a very creditable performance. Roland said it would have made a cat laugh to have seen Kirsty looking at the wall as if it were going to bite her and then heaving herself over it. Vanity was wearing a red rosette so I congratulated Sara and she told me she had won it in the hunter class.

While we were talking a lady came up and wished us all a hearty good afternoon. 'You did well with your little pony,' she announced. Then turning to Daddy she asked, 'Are you the father of these budding horsemen?'

Daddy looked amazed and muttered that he was.

'Got to have your permission, what!' stated the lady and proceeded to ignore Daddy and talk to Stuart. 'I've been watching you riding round with only one pony between the two of you for some time now and today is not the first time I've thought of lending you Meridian. Then I thought I'd wait and see what sort of show you put up today. Well I'm satisfied. You can ride him any time you like. Take him to graze with your animal or leave him at my place. I'll be responsible for any repairs to his tack, shoeing, etc.'

'What,' asked Roland, 'is Meridian?'

The lady looked at him as if he was an escaped lunatic and I heard her murmur her surprise at how long one pair of corduroy trousers lasted.

'Come over about ten tomorrow and you can try him.' She gave Kirsty a slap on the rump and marched away.

I gazed after her in dumb surprise. 'Did I hear right?' Stuart asked. 'Was she offering us a pony? Who on earth is she anyway?'

Sara said, laughing, 'If you could only have seen yourselves. You looked as if she was offering you a diamond mine. I rather think it will be her son's polo pony she was talking about. It has been out at grass since he was disabled. They used to have masses of horses but I think she keeps her hunters at livery with Captain Valeur now.'

'She's the lady in the red sports car,' I shouted. 'I knew I had seen her somewhere before.'

Stuart said in bemused tones, 'We'll have two ponies. No more altering stirrup leathers and split second timing and fighting over turns. I just can't believe it!'

Then the loudspeakers boomed across the show-ground announcing the winners of the jumping. Stuart was third and there was a flustered minute while Stuart tightened Kirsty's girths and trotted away. Mummy said while we had all been gossiping there had been another clear round and at the end of the jumping, a jump off for first and second place.

The first and second pones were both blood ponies and I felt terrifically proud of Kirsty as she cantered round the ring behind them. We all clapped like mad and Stuart had a struggle to keep a grin off his face when he rode past us.

We waited to see Vanity and Sara jump a clear round, then we repacked the bike and set off for home. It was my turn to ride Kirsty and as we trotted through Dunstan her green and red rosettes fluttered in the breeze. I had had the most wonderful day of my life. Kirsty was improving and tomorrow we would have two ponies. I could hardly believe our good luck.

Once we left Dunstan behind, I dismounted and Stuart pushed the bike, and as we made our way slowly homeward, I knew that tomorrow would be another step forward to the life I dreamt of when I could spend all my days with ponies.

These are other Knight Books

More books about horses and riding

Primrose Cumming
Four rode home

Monica Edwards
Rennie goes riding

Ruby Ferguson
Jill's gymkhana
A stable for Jill
Jill has two ponies
Jill and the perfect pony
Jill's riding club
Pony jobs for Jill
Rosettes for Jill
Jill enjoys her ponies
Jill's pony trek

Mary Treadgold
The Heron Ride
Return to the Heron

These are other Knight Books

Mary Treadgold
The Polly Harris

Mick and Caroline hated the idea of being cooped up in a city school. But that was before they lived in the forgotten riverside village, met the Prettyman's Hard Chaps, and became tangled up in a mystery which had them all baffled. Only after a wild chase across London, and finally up-river to the Polly Harris herself do Mick and Caroline learn the incredible story behind the many baffling clues they had tried to piece together during that winter term.

Ask your local bookseller, or at your public library, for details of other Knight Books, or write to the Editor-in-Chief, Knight Books, Arlen House, Salisbury Road, Leicester LE1 7QS.